Dying For Millions

For Robert

Dying For Millions

Judith Cutler

PIATKUS

First published in Great Britain in 1997 by
Judy Piatkus (Publishers) Ltd of
5 Windermill Street, London W1

This edition published 1997

A catalogue record for this book is available from the British Library

ISBN 0 7499 0403 8

Set in Times by
Intype London Ltd

Printed and bound in Great Britain by
Mackays of Chatham PLC, Chatham, Kent

Acknowledgements

I would like to thank the following for so generously giving me their time and expertise: Viv Oliver, who showed me round Coventry Airport on one of the coldest nights of the winter; Steve Smith, who proved that life as a roadie isn't all glamour; Graham Townshend, who would have sorted out Sophie's stomach as readily as he helped me with poisons; the Bee Gees, for all their years of music making.

Chapter One

One thing you can guarantee about Birmingham's Five Ways is the wind. With roads coming from five different directions I suppose it's likely that one of them will funnel any available breeze on to the car park, which is on top of a small shopping centre. In general I never have to park there: I leave my car – a new second-hand one – in the college car park and walk to the shops. Today, however, I had a double excuse: I had to collect my lap-top from Morgan's, where it was having its screen repaired; and I'd promised to drop Karen, a William Murdock student, as close as possible to the city centre, and her bus route. I'd been out to see her at her work experience placement, so it was natural for me to offer her a lift.

It would have been just as natural to throttle her, actually.

I'm not sure whether it was what she was saying or how she was saying it. Whatever configuration of the nasal passages – or is it the chest cavity? – that produce the voice's timbre had given Karen a particularly irritating squeak, and she'd grafted on to her native Brummie accent an Australian-sounding lift at the end of each sentence, which made even the simplest statement a fierce interrogation. Too much 'Neighbours' and 'Home and Away', I suppose.

'We're having exams at the end of this *term*? *Right*?'

'Yes,' I said. Was I supposed to justify the college's unreasonable evaluation methods or simply give her the dates?

'But it's so close to *Easter*?'

'We always have end-of-term exams. Ah!' I spotted a space.

'You can get in *there*?'

To be honest, there aren't many spaces into which I can't persuade my little Renault. But this one was big enough to take a small bus, and there was no likelihood of her having to climb out through the sun-roof.

It was easier simply to reverse in than to explain. In normal circumstances my rear bumper would have ended up no more than two inches from the armco barrier. But Karen had insisted on putting her surprisingly large bag in the boot, so I had to allow enough room for the tailgate to swing. I could understand perfectly why her temporary employers should have decided that they could release her an hour early today.

There! Beautifully parallel to and equidistant from the white lines. Satisfied with that at least, I was out and opening the tailgate before I realised just how gusty it was. 'Just stay there a moment, Karen,' I said, suddenly aware of the pile of vulnerable papers on the back seat. There were employers' reports on students and – more inflammatory – students' reports on employers; those especially were highly confidential. 'No! Don't try to get out yet!'

'Oh, it's all *right*?'

But it wasn't.

A malicious flourish of wind swirled the lot out through her door, my frantic efforts to slam the tailgate making matters even worse.

There they were, spreading themselves thinly across the tarmac, darting away from me like minnows from a pike. Karen thought it best behoved her to stand and watch. Perhaps she was right. I told myself I was fielding to save a Test Match and darted and ducked, despite my thirty-six years, snatching from the jaws of disaster. But one page headed purposefully, inexorably, for the shelter of a regrettable piece of American automobile engineering – parked with scant respect, incidentally, for the recognised parking order. It claimed sanctuary near the rear axle and regarded me balefully as I half-knelt in entreaty.

Karen eventually joined me, out of breath after no more

then a light jog. She'd picked up a few papers, and thrust them at me.

'I've got to catch my *bus*? I've got to get home early this *avvo*?'

Did she mean 'afternoon'? 'Right,' I said. 'You get your bus and I'll stay and grovel to the owner of this monstrosity.'

'Why d'you have to grovel to me?' asked a voice, produced by entirely congenial nasal passages and a wonderful chest cavity.

It would have been poetic if I could have turned, got up and thrown myself into his arms in one eloquent movement. But it was not to be. My knee seized halfway up, and all I could do was flail awkwardly until he shot out a hand to steady me and haul me to my feet. But I ended up in his arms.

No, this was no Mills and Boon encounter. Just the return of my cousin Andy to his native city.

I hugged him, laughing, then pushed him away. 'What the hell are you doing driving a gas-guzzler like this?'

'It's Tobe's. What the hell were you doing kneeling worshipping it?'

'And what are you doing in Brum without letting me know? The gig isn't till the end of the week.'

'Been checking out the Music Centre,' he said.

That didn't quite explain his presence at Five Ways, but no doubt he had his reasons. And the more you asked Andy, the less he was likely to tell. You had to wait for the moment when he chose to be expansive.

'Where's Ruth?' I asked. Ruth was his new wife, something of a surprise to many. Andy had been going out with an air-head with big hair, but had suddenly and completely fallen in love with her aunt, a headmistress of about forty.

'Back home in Devon. She picked up a nasty bug in Vienna. Wonderful – she swans round the worst refugee camps in Africa as if there were no such things as germs and when she gets back to civilisation she gets the first thing on offer.'

'So where are you staying?' By rights it should be with me. Andy always stays with me, but usually has the grace to fix it before he arrives in Birmingham.

'With you?'

There seemed to be a slight note of doubt in his voice; or perhaps I was just too sensitive today.

'I should bloody hope so!'

'Look – I've got a couple of things to see to first. Would it mess you up if I turned up later – say, ten? Could you book us in somewhere?' It was unlike Andy to concern himself with such trivialities as my convenience: Ruth was undoubtedly house-training him. This business of checking out a venue suggested a new punctiliousness too.

'There's a new restaurant attached to the Indian take-away,' I said promptly. If he could be efficient, so could I. 'Now, what about that report?'

I stepped back to let him open the car door and trod hard on a foot. Karen's. I'd had no idea she was still there; I'd vaguely assumed she had gone off for her bus. I turned to apologise profusely but from the glazed look on her face she might have been one of those religious fanatics who are above pain. Disregarding a temptation to stamp on the other one to test this theory, I realised I had another apology to make. I hadn't introduced her to Andy.

I slapped the car's flank, and gestured. Obligingly, he got out with a smile – slightly cooler from the one he'd given me, but perhaps she wouldn't notice. I introduced them, and he chatted easily: suspecting, I suppose, from long experience of dealing with teenage fans, that she'd be tongue-tied. Then, before she noticed, he'd retrieved the paper and given it to me, bidden her a cheery farewell, and driven off.

Poor kid. She was blushing so hard she was almost in tears.

'Oh, Sophie,' she said at last, 'wasn't he *lovely*? I mean, his *hands*? Hasn't he got lovely *hands*? And those *eyes*? Did you ever see such lovely blue *eyes*? And his *teeth*?'

I let her ramble on: she wasn't particularly discerning in her list. I think Andy would have done better to have had a brace when I had mine, and although he was now as anti-smoking as my friend George had been, the years of tobacco fumes had undoubtedly aged his skin; other, less legal, substances had also taken their toll. Certainly he now looked older than me rather than nine months younger. His hair was thinning, too, but was at last beginning to respond to Ruth's regimen of kinder colouring and more conditioner. His cheekbones, though, I did envy. Andy had the sort of face that would age down to fine bones and interesting angles.

'. . . *photograph*?' Karen was saying.

'Photograph? Of you together?'

'Oh, Sophie! Could you? Would he?' She was ready to cry.

'I'll see what I can do. Perhaps when he's back in Brum for his gig. I didn't realise you were a fan of his.' Surely she was the wrong age for Andy Rivers: I'd have expected her to be worshipping Oasis, or whoever.

'My mum always has been. She says his music has *tunes*? And – I mean, he's just so good-looking! He's *bad* – absolutely *wicked*.' This time she sighed on the last word in each sentence of what I assumed was the highest praise.

I considered. To me he'd always been just Andy, someone to tease and teach alternately. My father, who coached me at cricket, had always refused to pass on to Andy the secrets of good slow bowling, on the grounds that he was too idle to learn, so it was from me that Andy had acquired a leg-break so devilish that Warwickshire had selected him for the Colts team. They'd been talking about apprenticeships and professional contracts before he whizzed off to Spain at the age of seventeen. Since the family had insisted that he should become a plumber, I suppose it was his way of cutting a Gordian knot.

'Don't *you* think he's *gorgeous*?' she prompted me, irate.

'But he's my cousin, you see,' I said inadequately.

'*You're* his *cousin*?' Her disbelief was so exquisitely unflattering I couldn't help laughing. 'But what are you doing – I mean—'

'What am I doing being a college lecturer when he's doing something so very much more exciting? That's how it is, in real life.'

'But shouldn't you – you know, be working for him?'

I shook my head, laughing. 'Oh, Karen – Andy's got everything! How could *I* possibly do anything to help *him*?'

If anyone needed help, it was clearly me. I was kneeling on my living room floor, trying to match sets of mud-stained sheets of paper. One, which contained well-documented allegations of racist and sexist behaviour by a well-known city firm of solicitors, bore a large thumb-print which might well have been Andy's. I put it to one side; clearly I'd need to talk to my boss about the contents, and discuss them at length with the student, which would mean yet another lunch-hour consumed by college business. I was beginning to see this job in terms of missed meal-breaks; indeed, missed meals. I had to make my visits at times convenient to the employers but also without disrupting any of my own classes. Since the number of hours a week all the college staff were required to teach had suddenly and mysteriously gone up by ten per cent, this made balancing the two factors extremely tricky unless I was prepared to discount my own needs entirely. I certainly couldn't have done it at all without a car, a form of transport I'd managed to eschew for several years, preferring a combination of cycle and public transport. But I'd been forced to make a virtue of necessity.

Nine-thirty: time to gather the whole lot up. There didn't seem to be anything missing.

The doorbell rang.

It took me longer to struggle to my feet than I liked. My right knee, affronted by an injury last Easter, occasionally chose to lock if it thought I was maltreating it, and it was beginning to regard sitting on the floor with disfavour. The bell rang again.

'Andy! Why didn't you let yourself in?' He usually rang and unlocked the door at the same time.

'Thought you'd got company.' He gestured: his thumb curled towards my car.

'My new toy,' I said proudly.

He stepped past me to dump an overnight case in the hall, and then turned. 'Show me.'

Huddling against the cold night air, I led the way down the drive. I'd extolled the virtues of half the key features when I dwindled to a halt; this was a man who drove a BMW when he wasn't borrowing his wife's Mercedes.

'Why did you buy this model?' he asked.

I'd have been tempted, with any other multi-millionaire, to snap that it was because I was bored with my Rolls. But to Andy I told the truth. 'D'you remember Aggie?' I began.

'You don't forget the Aggies of this world,' he said. 'I've brought her some genuine Devon clotted cream: I'll take it round in a minute.'

'Well, Aggie's daughter had just bought it. Then she won a better model in a competition – she wins things all the time, holidays, hampers, and this is the second time she's won a car – so I bought it from her.'

He nodded as if impressed.

'I thought we'd take it to the restaurant,' I said. 'Less obtrusive than that thing of yours.'

'Tobe's,' he said.

'Tobe's,' I agreed. 'Why not your own?'

'Had a bit of a scrape,' he said. 'How long's that house been empty?'

I blinked at the snub; it was unlike Andy to be edgy. 'The one opposite? Six months or so. They cut their losses and left. Aggie reckons someone's going to rent it. The couple in the next house'll be glad of some company – they're pretty frail . . . Are you all right?'

'Feeling the cold in these northern climes.' He grinned reassuringly. 'Let's go back in. Then I'll have a pee and we'll go and eat.'

The restaurant wasn't licensed so I fished a four-pack of lager out from the pantry. Andy eyed it. 'Why don't I drive your car so you can drink?'

'You're off booze?'

'For a bit. Until I – for a bit.'

I looked at him sharply, but he had already picked up his case and was heading towards his bedroom.

It took him a few minutes to deliver the cream to my next-door neighbour and then we set off. He was in vegetarian mode again, after a summer as a carnivore. I didn't comment: after a stint working at the African hospital financed by his trust fund, he often ate frugally. He wasn't ostentatious about it, or about giving up alcohol, which he also did from time to time – no one could ever tell from his behaviour at parties that he wasn't genuinely tipsy on nothing stronger than mineral water.

'Channa's excellent,' he said, gesturing with a piece of garlic nan.

'So's my biryani,' I replied, spearing a prawn.

We both smiled at Ahmed, the waiter, who had come not to be sycophantic but to enquire, as he always did, how we were getting on. It was my approval, not Andy's, he was seeking; I was a valued regular, a customer long before the take-away spawned the restaurant, and Andy was valuable as a friend of mine, not as an international megastar – even if he recognised him as such. Ahmed smiled on us almost equally and withdrew. He soon returned with a jug of water.

'You forgot to ask, dear,' he said.

'I knew I wouldn't need to, Ahmed,' I said.

He winked, and went off to seat some new customers.

Andy doodled on the tablecloth with his index finger. 'I'm giving it up, Sophie. Music. Well, the music business.'

'Permanently? I thought you said something about a sabbatical—'

'Don't want to make too much of a big deal over this gig. Too bloody emotional as it is, the last gig in a tour. Hope Ruth'll be well enough to come up.' He broke some nan, scooped a mouthful of dhal. 'You know, for the party afterwards – you'll be there?'

'Try and keep me away. Shall I bring someone?' Chris, the policeman with whom I had an on-off relationship, might be up from Bramshill for the weekend.

'Thought you might like to see who you could pull. There's always Duck.'

Duck might be one of the best lighting engineers in Europe but he had a walk like Lady Thatcher's and halitosised for England.

'Gee, thanks.' Time to change the subject: he'd give me a fistful of passes anyway. Perhaps I could give Karen one – and her mother. I topped up my lager. 'Mwandara's got to you, has it?'

'Not just the hospital – the whole of the country. Well,

the Third World in general, to be honest. Jesus, Sophie – the waste, the poverty, the corruption, the sheer indifference . . . I have to do something.' All the laughlines had solidified into frustrated anger.

I nodded; I'd seen it coming. 'Aren't you more use to Mwandara as a pop star attracting attention and funds than as just another pair of hands – unskilled hands at that?'

'I shan't be spending any more time there. Not as a field worker, anyway. UNICEF have asked me to become a goodwill ambassador. Yes, despite my past! Don't forget – I've been squeaky-clean for years now.' He smiled ironically, but he had reason to be proud of himself. He'd probably succumbed to all the temptations going, and invented a few more along the way, but he'd come through it all and if he looked back he never showed it, even to me. He'd gone further, been prominent in campaigns against drugs ever since he'd dried out. Some people said he was like a younger Cliff Richard in zealousness – though without the religious bit, I was relieved to say. His crusading image didn't fit his music: once a violent, primitive rock – though always, as Karen's mother had rightly observed, with an accessible melody – and nowadays a much more sophisticated affair, with lots of African rhythms. Nelson Mandela was known to be a fan, and had attended the opening of the township cricket club which had asked Andy to be its Patron.

'Will you miss it? The music, I mean?'

'Some of it. The roar of the grease-paint, the smell of the crowd . . . Same as you'd miss teaching, I suppose.' Suddenly he yawned, showing all those expensively capped teeth. 'No, no coffee for me, thanks. Sophie?'

'Sophie doesn't drink it at this time of night,' said Ahmed paternally, giving me the bill.

Chapter Two

Andy was hurtling along imaginary roads on my exercise bike when I took a mug of tea into him the next morning. He was also singing along to the radio, sharing Robert Merrill's baritone part in the famous duet from Bizet's *Pearlfishers*; his voice was still pleasing, if huskier these days. He peered at the tea, as if suspicious, but grinned when he saw it was milkless.

I was about to apologise – I never seem to remember to put the milk in the fridge.

'No, I prefer it like that. Remember that diet I was telling you about? It's best to avoid milk when you're on it. Don't know why – can't be bothered with the philosophy. Just know it works.'

He certainly looked well. He'd never been anything other than slender, apart from during his early twenties, when he was drinking as if he expected them to ration it. But now muscles showed finely under healthy skin. You certainly wouldn't have guessed he was just concluding a gruelling world tour.

I thought of my own body, dull-skinned and flabby after a jogging-less, knee-troubled couple of months, and made a note, when I wasn't late for work, to ask him more about his diet. It wouldn't be today, though. Before I got home, he'd be back to Devon and Ruth.

'See you Friday, then? At the airport?'

He shook his head. 'It'll be more like Saturday, and I'll get a taxi. I'll let myself in.'

'Breakfast?'

He shook his head extravagantly.

'Lemon tea at eleven?'

'Some bloke's missing a good wife.'

'Sexist bastard. Well, I'm off to earn my crust.'

He stopped pedalling and slipped off the bike. A sweaty hug, and a tiny kiss on the lips. That was the routine.

Taking the car into work always generated a mixture of guilt and frustration. I knew I was adding not just to city pollution levels but also to global warming, and I could see quite clearly the effect of extra cars – one-driver, no-passenger cars – on a grievously overloaded road system. Any day now the city would be gridlocked. But today I really needed the car to make another visit, this time to an airport – not Birmingham International, but West Midlands, a small-scale airport where I hoped to place some students. This meant heading out along the A38 via Spaghetti Junction. It was fortunate I had a class till ten: it would allow a little time for the roads to clear.

The motorways into the city were still clogged, but the outward routes, including the A38 Lichfield Road, were clear. There was a slight delay on the Tyburn Road, where a milk-float had somehow spilt its entire load, but eventually I picked up the road to the airport just after the turning for Minworth sewage works. In cold, wet weather like this, there was no smell to betray it; I wouldn't have taken bets on it after a long, hot summer, though.

It was surprisingly easy to get in. I'd expected security guards – but then, it was a public airport. I found my way to a small visitors' car park near the administration block. Mine was easily the smallest car, but I compensated by making it the most neatly parked. I brushed myself down, and headed for Reception.

In addition to the car, the new job had also called for a few changes in my wardrobe: gone were the days when I had merely to decide which pair of jeans to wear. I had had to lose street cred in order to gain credibility with employers. And, perhaps, there was a faint but enduring hope that one of them might one day realise how efficient and professional

I was and head-hunt me from the wilting grove of Academe that was William Murdock. I still enjoyed the teaching, and all the pastoral work with the students, but a brief sojourn at another, better-endowed college, had made me realise the advantages of working in a pleasant environment.

Although the administrative block was a low and unimpressive building one grade up from a pre-fab, the doors opened – then shut – automatically, admitting me to a newly-decorated and clean foyer. I was greeted by a motherly middle-aged receptionist who appeared genuinely sorry when she told me that Mark Winfield, the Training Officer I'd come to see, was delayed in a meeting. She brought me current magazines and newly-made tea – with fresh milk – and settled me in a comfortable chair. I wallowed in the unexpected luxury of a break. I flicked through this month's *Cosmopolitan*: my horoscope promised a change in my fortunes by the end of the month and warned me not to let my independence discourage my partner. Partner, indeed! The nearest thing I had to a partner was Chris, now on some course which seemed likely to whizz him from his current rank of DCI to something way beyond superintendent in less than no time. And the higher he flew, the less likely we were to agree.

'Ms Rivers?'

I jumped, but had the presence of mind to stand up and offer my hand. 'Sophie, please.'

'Mark Winfield,' said the young man, taking it and shaking it warmly. He was in a suit considerably flasher than mine, but his hair was well styled and his complexion lightly tanned. He was about thirty. 'Now, how may I help you? Work experience, I think you said in your letter—'

'For my students,' I said. 'I'm responsible for placing them in organisations like yours where they can get some idea of the world of work.'

'For how long are we talking about?'

I was slightly puzzled: I'd have expected this conversation to take place in his office. 'Usually a week, occasionally two or three weeks. Some placements prefer to use them on a range of jobs: others prefer shadowing – following you around all day, about your daily round.'

He gave an exaggerated shudder. 'You mean, they follow you *everywhere*?'

'Apart from the loo, yes. Not just set-piece meetings – all the behind-closed-door politicking as well.'

He wrinkled a straight, rather elegant nose. 'There's a lot of confidential stuff in a place like this. After all the problems other airports have had with demonstrators, we wouldn't want to take any chances.' He turned slightly – we were about to move at last.

'Are you involved in live animal transportation, then?' I asked, gathering up my bag and preparing to follow wherever he led.

'Not now. The management saw the way things were going and pulled out before the publicity started. There's plenty of other lucrative contracts without actively looking for trouble.' He led the way, limping slightly on his left leg. I hoped it wasn't just the cut of his suit that gave him such broad shoulders.

I followed him to a door. He tapped numbers into a keyboard, shielded so that only the most determinedly curious could have worked out the code, then held the door open for me.

'You know, of course, that we don't handle large numbers of passengers here. We're almost exclusively freight with some short-haul private passenger flights. STOLs – short take off and landing. You see the Dash Sevens over there? That sort of thing. There are training flights, too. And over there is the helipad.'

I nodded; I would have to check out all the details later so I could use the right lingo – and, more importantly, understand should he use it. 'You mean, like the airport in Docklands?' I said brightly.

He stopped by another door, again secretively tapping in a code before ushering me through.

'We're less busy than they are. Like I said, it's mostly freight. The container base is over there.' He pointed through triple-glazed windows. 'Customs and Excise. Engineering. Control tower.'

'You're quite a small concern.' I hoped I didn't sound disparaging.

'But very efficient. We have to be, there are so few of us. Most of the clerical work is now computerised and as soon as a plane is logged through Air Traffic Control it triggers a print-out in the accounts office. Which is where your students could be most useful.' He gave a bark of laughter. 'Symbiosis – isn't that what they call it? You want us to give them experience; we'd want to get some work out of them.'

I hesitated: work experience placements weren't intended to turn students into unpaid labourers. 'What sort of work?'

'Quite responsible. The sort that might lead to paid work later – temporary relief when staff are off sick or on training. We're very forward-looking in our training policies. Investors in People.'

I smiled. 'It's on your letter heading.'

'Right! Some of it's essential – propellers are lethal things. We don't want people walking into them. And planes come expensive. Apart from that, we try to ensure everyone has their skills up-dated as often as possible. Not just those skills which would immediately benefit the company, either. Languages. Fitness. And we have regular team-building weekends at outdoor activity centres.'

The tone of his voice suggested he was particularly proud of something which I've always considered anathema. Imagine it – a weekend being swung from the end of a wet rope by a boss you couldn't swear at . . .

'So how could our students help? In the short term, that is?'

For answer he took me out of his office, back into the corridor: another code-controlled door, this time into an office. From the windows you could see an immense aircraft sitting on the runway, disgorging containers. There was, I suppose, some background noise from the trucks and the plane itself, but nothing outrageous enough to disturb two women who were tapping at computer keyboards like creatures possessed. Their area was sectioned off by sound-screens, forming a self-contained enclave.

'This is where the usual secretarial stuff is done.' He stopped by the section nearest the door. 'Morning, Sal – how's Kieran?'

'Still teething. Especially at three in the morning.'

'Ron doing his share?'
'When he remembers.'
'Make sure he does!'
I wasn't sure how to take that little exchange. It seemed genuine, but I'm always suspicious of public displays designed to show what a brilliant, caring employer you are. I smiled sympathetically at Sal, who smiled back without any hint of irony. Perhaps he *was* simply a good manager.
'Tell me,' Winfield began, 'how flexible your students would be in their working hours.'
'They'd normally do the same as everyone else – nine till five.'
'Ah. That limits us slightly. You see, we're at our busiest between the hours of nine and twelve.' He paused for effect. 'In the evening.'
'Is that why it's so quiet now? I'd expected to be yelling over the sound of incoming or outgoing aircraft.'
'That's right.' He guided me to a window. 'See, it's mostly training flights during the day. I suppose you don't fly yourself?' His voice changed; I had an enthusiast on my hands.
I watched a smallish aircraft bounce to an awkward halt. If it were me, I'd want to loop and dive; but then, I reminded myself sourly, I wouldn't be able to. 'I get vertigo,' I said.
'So do I, on the ground. But never up there. I've even done parachute jumps! You should learn. Think about it!' When he smiled his face was transformed.
I reflected briefly on the use flying would be to a woman from semi-detached Harborne with a job that consumed lunch-times and weekends like a gull gobbled fish. But I did feel a nasty yearning. And if Andy was learning to fly a helicopter, why shouldn't I? No. For him flying made absolute sense. For me?
'One day, maybe,' I said, non-committally. Then I found myself smiling back and adding, 'Actually, I should love to.' What I had to do was direct the conversation back to education and the needs of my students – tactfully for preference. 'When did you learn? Were you an air cadet or something?'
'Fire Service, actually. That's how I got involved in training.'

'That sounds an unusual career path!'

He laughed. 'I was responsible for health and safety. And as I said, an airport is a dangerous place – you should see it at night when we're busy with all the Parcel Force traffic. Planes and lorries. Someone had to take responsibility for all the casual staff we've got out there and when I hurt my hip – oh, I fell through a roof – the company offered to take me on. Good of them. New General Manager – very enlightened. Anyway, since I started, there have only been a couple of incidents, neither of them serious. Whereas before, we were beginning to have trouble getting insurance.'

'You must be doing a good job.'

'We all work hard here. Which brings me back to your students.' He'd taken the hint. 'They'd have to have a serious capacity for hard work. I don't want anyone farting round thinking all they have to do is make tea and do their nails. Real work is what I'm talking.' Take it or leave it, his voice said: then that smile.

'And not nine till five? That would eliminate some of our Asian students – the girls, especially. Their fathers bring them in at five to nine, collect them at four-thirty.'

'What about the others? You must have other students?'

'Plenty.' My tone conveyed more conviction than I felt. How many students would want to work those hours?

'I think there might be a way round this,' he said slowly. 'What about – the same day a week, for several weeks? We could train them up to do something worthwhile, and it would free one of our staff to undertake a period of training. Then, as I said, there'd be the possibility of doing relief or holiday work, but that would almost certainly involve several evenings a week.'

I back-tracked. 'A lot of students do evening work at McDonald's, or delivering pizzas. I'm sure we'll find you someone good.'

'I don't want anyone who *isn't* good!' His smile again, eventually, softened his words. 'Oh, and we need two written references – Department of Transport regulations.' He shot a look at his watch. 'Twelve already. You'll join me for a bite in the canteen?'

I looked at mine in turn. 'I wish I could. But I'm teaching at one-fifteen.'

'Come on. It's only fifteen minutes back to the city centre. Well, twenty.'

His smile became very engaging indeed. I shouldn't offend a potential placement; it would have been churlish to refuse. 'I promised I'd talk to a student – can I make a phone call to put her off?'

'There's a phone in my office.'

It turned out Mark had played cricket before he hurt his hip, and was still a keen Warwickshire supporter. So we gossiped cricket for as long as it took us to eat salad and rolls, and drink rather weak decaffeinated coffee in what he referred to as the Mess. I was the only woman among short-haired men in smart shirts with impressive shoulder flashes; braided caps were much in evidence.

'I'm sorry,' I said at last, 'but I really must dash. I've got an A-level class.'

'Tell you what,' he said, 'you really ought to see what it's like at night. Come over next week. Let's see – I think I'm rostered for Tuesday. Come over about nine. We'll have a drink first, then I'll show you round.'

I must have been off my head: trailing round in the cold – and almost certainly the rain – of a February night wasn't my usual idea of a good time. But I heard myself agreeing. And, come to think of it, I found myself looking forward to it.

Chapter Three

RIVERS, ANDREW MICHAEL. *Passed away in his sleep, 14 February. Reunited with his dear wife Freya. Private funeral. No flowers.*

I'd been leafing idly through the courtesy *Evening Mail* at the Chinese takeaway. In the kitchen, someone added garlic to a pan; two middle-aged men were condoling with each other on West Bromwich Albion's recent bad performance.

– *Passed away in his sleep*—

'Two frie' ri'e; chicken and bean sprou'; beef with green pepper?'

No! No, not Andy. Someone else. Andrew Rivers was a common enough name. This Andrew Rivers *couldn't* be my cousin Andy. I'd know the moment he died, without having to read about it in a evening paper. I'd *know.*

'Don't use their heads, see. All those lofted balls . . .'

– *dear wife Freya*—

I forced myself to look at the TV on the corner of the counter, but they'd turned the sound down. The decor, then: I tried to concentrate on the tasselled lanterns and what seemed to be a shrine next to the till.

But my eyes wouldn't focus, and when I closed the paper firmly my hands opened it again. *Andrew Robert Rivers . . .*

'Szechuan chicken and plai' ri'e?'

It didn't make sense.

'Szechuan chicken and plai' ri'e?'

'Isn't that yours, love?' someone asked.

Embarrassed, I got to my feet, left the paper on the formica table, and collected my food.

I rarely drank spirits before a meal, but this time I left the containers on the hob to keep warm while I sank a large slug of Jameson's. The sensible thing was to phone Andy, just to make sure everything was all right, but the logical part of my brain was outraged. Of course everything was all right!

But it wasn't. OK, Andy Rivers was not an unusual name – but Freya certainly was. In fact, I only knew one other, the teenage daughter of a friend. Andy had married his Freya when he was eighteen and into serious mistakes. She'd been a wispy girl, limp and pallid in the high-waisted, floating dresses already going out of vogue, and doing nothing in particular. I'd tried to love her, for Andy's sake, but was relieved when after a couple of years she drifted off with a colleague of Andy's further up the success ladder and into proportionately heavier drugs. She died of some bizarre drug cocktail before she reached her twenty-fifth birthday. Andy was by then deep into another relationship, but Freya's death had shocked him into giving up even coffee. For a while, at least.

The whiskey did little more than fuddle my thinking, so I emptied the rest of the glass down the sink and put the bottle away. To stop myself thinking about the notice, I watched the news while I ate. As soon as it was over, however, I was into worry-mode again. Clearly Andy was alive and well – the whole nation would have heard Michael Buerk breaking the news otherwise – but I was still uneasy. I reached for my 'Do Tomorrow' pad: Phone the *Evening Mail* and check the provenance of the death notice.

And then I phoned Andy anyway. To ask after Ruth, naturally.

'Bloody virus,' she whispered. 'All those years teaching – you'd have thought my throat would be made of leather.'

Her voice stopped abruptly.

'She's supposed to be Trappist for the next week,' said Andy, trying not to sound anxious but failing to sound amused. 'So she won't be coming over to Dublin for the gig there. That's for definite.'

'What about the Music Centre?' Surely nothing would stop her missing that.

'Yeah. A bit of a milestone, isn't it?'

'I can't imagine it without her. Couldn't she come along to the party and gesture? It's about all most of us can do after that level of decibels.'

'We'll do what the medics say. Only thing.' His voice was sombre.

After that, I didn't mention the ad. *Sufficient unto the day is the evil thereof . . .*

The girl I phoned at the *Evening Mail* was adamant. There was a procedure for checking that notices placed by phone were valid, and it was always enforced. No one on the phone desk ever authorised a small ad without phoning back to make sure the caller was *bona fide*.

'Never?'

'*Never*. We simply won't accept the item if someone's calling from a phone box. We'd want an office number if they weren't calling from home. We actually prefer the information to be faxed.'

'So if I wanted to let you know I was engaged—'

'Ooh, congratulations! Not many people bother these days—'

'Which I'm not, you'd make sure my putative fiancé endorsed it?'

'Of course.'

I thanked her humbly, aware that I was wasting her time.

And mine; I looked at my watch. I'd better try to match the vacancy at the airport with the students wanting work experience. But before that, there was a session on Joyce – *A Painful Case*. And after that, at the beginning of my lunch-break, the meeting with Richard Jeffries, my boss, about those allegations of racism.

Richard was about eight weeks away from premature retirement. The economy drive which had led to the staff teaching all those extra hours had also been aimed at middle-aged and senior staff, encouraging them with the prospect of redundancy payments or pension enhancement to go well before they reached sixty. Richard had embraced the offer with fervour, even if the financial climate was too inequitable to allow him to fulfil his dream of setting up a small bookshop in Hay-on-Wye. Nonetheless, on the calendar hung by his desk – tasteful portraits of steam locomotives – he'd crossed out every day passed since Christmas, like a prisoner waiting for parole. If you looked closely you could see that a little figure had been pencilled in over each date: he was now on retirement minus fifty-six or thereabouts.

'You really think there's something in this lot?' he said wearily, flicking through the student's report on her apparently lecherous temporary employer.

'Enough to make me want to talk to Naheeda.'

'You haven't yet?' Behind his glasses, hope that she'd deny everything glimmered briefly.

'She's off sick at the moment.'

'Genuine?' He was getting interested. 'Or doesn't she want you to ask her questions?'

'I suppose it's genuine.' I hadn't given it much thought. No doubt that was why people like Richard got to be boss.

'Might be worth popping round to find out.' Relief: he could postpone making a decision. 'When you've got time, that is.' He was begging me to tell him I was too busy. Couldn't I leave it, he was asking, until some young Turk had taken his job? Then I could go ahead and discover all sorts of nastiness, take all sorts of high-profile action. But couldn't it wait eight weeks?

I relented. 'I'm pretty busy at the moment. Up to my eyes with this work experience business.'

'Don't let it do to you what it did to Tim.'

Tim was my predecessor. He'd been pressed to continue just a little longer, though he'd dearly have loved to retire to his hand-painted narrowboat – and had been rushed to hospital just after Christmas with a burst duodenal ulcer.

'Any news?'

'He's leaving, of course. Premature retirement on the

grounds of ill health. Do you know, I haven't even been to see him,' he said, ashamed.

'You're pretty busy yourself.' Not that any of us lower orders liked to think management ever did anything.

'Tell you something,' he said, lowering his voice and looking around him as if he feared the room might be bugged, 'I'm counting the days till I go.'

And he couldn't understand when I started to laugh.

I was still grinning to myself when I turned the corner of the corridor leading to my fifteenth floor staff room and ran slap into Gurjit, a tall, elegant Sikh student returning consistently high grades for all her A-level subjects. She'd just passed her driving test and been rewarded by a Clio like mine – but not a second-hand one. Her parents had made a point of coming to our otherwise poorly-attended parents' evenings, and had made it clear that they would support Gurjit in anything that would improve her prospects of university and a subsequent job. What about the airport work experience opportunity for Gurjit? Her car would enable her to travel backwards and forwards safely in the dark, and I was sure her earnestness would score highly with Mark Winfield.

'I'd have to discuss it with my parents,' she said slowly. 'But in principle it seems an excellent idea.'

I beamed: not many students used phrases like 'in principle' these days.

'Did you have any dates in mind, Sophie? I wouldn't want it to clash with my assignments.'

There was so much invested in her, wasn't there?

'Working only one day or evening a week should mean your assignments don't suffer.' I said, as enthusiastically as if the whole idea had been mine, not Mark's. 'In any case, we're very flexible here – most people would give you an extension if you needed it. And,' I added, mentally clinching it, 'you may get some material you can use for your Computer Studies project – you know you have to do one in your second year.'

She nodded. 'I will have to discuss it with my parents and confirm it—'

'By Monday, please. If you don't want the placement, I must offer it to someone else straight away.'

She nodded. 'I understand. Excuse me, Sophie – I have to see Mr Jagger. He's promised to help me with my criminal law.'

Everyone else called him Mick, of course, even the principal. If only she could relax . . .

I was just unwrapping a canteen sandwich which insisted it was cheese and salad when Karen drifted into the staff room. This is not a common room, where staff can let their hair down, but a work room and office combined, occupied by a dozen staff constantly summoned by three phones and invaded by a steady trickle of students, none of whom ever feel the need to knock.

'Is it all *right*? About the *photograph*?'

'Photograph? Oh, you mean you and Andy.' A bit of cucumber – in fact, as I subsequently discovered, the only bit of cucumber – came adrift and slithered down my blouse.

'The concert's *the day after tomorrow*?'

So it was. Dublin this evening for a TV interview, the Dublin gig tomorrow evening and a midnight flight into Birmingham: then the Music Centre gig on Saturday evening.

'I'll talk to him on Saturday, Karen.'

'But the concert's *on Saturday*? And it's *sold out*?'

From the day booking opened. 'So neither you nor your mum can get in?'

'Mum can,' she said. 'And she won't give me her *ticket*?' She looked at me, demanding sympathy.

I resisted a strong impulse to say, 'I should hope not!' and bent my brain to more positive solutions. Andy would give her a pass, without question, and probably one for the party afterwards – plus one for her mother. But I don't like to see my students getting something for nothing when with only a little effort they could get a lot more.

'Are you any good at washing-up?' I asked.

'*Washing up*?'

'Mmm. They always want teams of washers-up back stage.

It's not an exciting job, but everyone knows it isn't so a lot of people come and talk to you. Not just the roadies and the caterers, but wives and children of the band.'

A spasm of disgust crossed her face. '*Wives*? *Children*?'

What else did she expect?

'And the backing singers. And Andy always makes a point of going round to say thank you. You and your mum might get a pass to go to the party afterwards.'

'*Mum*?' More disgust.

'You'd be able to introduce her to Andy,' I said diplomatically; what I actually had in mind was that Mum would be able to curb any possible teenage excesses. 'I hope she won't faint!' Karen did not smile. 'Shall I fix it for you? There'll probably be free food to take home, too. I got roped in for a Phil Collins gig and I fed my friends for a week on stuff that would otherwise have been thrown away.'

'Would I – really – get to talk to *him*? *Really*?' Her voice was suddenly intense; I could have sworn she went pale.

'If I can get you in, I'm sure you'll get to talk to him. And I'll take a photo of you together. *If*. Shall I try?' I reached for the phone. 'It'll be a long day, but apart from anything else you'll be able to put it on your CV.'

I got through to Ollie, a mate of Tobe's: one of the Brum roadies, as opposed to those that toured with Andy's show. Ollie was apparently eating crisps in a very loud pub, but recognised my voice.

'Hi, our Soph! Nice to hear you. How's old Andy? What's this about him and this bird?'

'What bird?'

'The professor old enough to be his mum?'

'She was a teacher and she's a couple of years older than me!'

'Funny business, all the same.'

I didn't want to comment, and rushed straight in with the question of Karen.

'No probs. Me missus'll show her the ropes. Tell her to wear, you know, sensible stuff. Phiz is on and we don't want to give him too many ideas, do we? The missus could meet her outside nice and early. OK?'

'How early? Half-eight?' Although the question was for Ollie, I looked at Karen.

Karen nodded. If it meant meeting Andy she'd be there at dawn, her eyes implied.

Eleven o'clock. I sat drearily over a pile of essays which didn't seem to get any smaller.

The trouble was, I always put to the bottom of the pile those by people who hadn't any ideas, or whose handwriting was illegible, and inevitably I lived to regret it. I decided to give up, pour a finger of Jameson's, and retire with *Middlemarch* to the bath. I'd got no further than packing away the marking, however, when the phone rang.

'Sophie?'

Andy!

'How's Dublin?'

'Wet and windy. Don't know why I came over early – the RTE interview was crap. I could have stayed with Ruth till tomorrow.'

'And you can't even phone her to have a moan in case she starts talking?' That at least explained his phone call to me: he wanted someone to natter to.

'Right. I just told her I was OK and hung up. Lead us not into temptation.'

'It's that bad?'

'No one knows what it is. They've done swabs and everything. Nothing bacterial. I even wondered about having a shrink see her, in case it's psychosomatic, but that means her having to break the vow of silence.'

'Any other symptoms?' Not that I was a doctor – I was just interested. And it struck me as odd that he should even consider a psychiatrist at this stage.

'A general malaise. She gets tired very quickly. No fever, nothing you can put your finger on.' His voice was tight with anxiety. At last he changed gear: 'And how are you? You sounded a bit stressed last night.'

'I'm fine!' I tried to keep my voice light. 'What about you?'

'I'm fine too.'

So neither of us was.
'Talk?' I said.
'When I see you.'
Very far from fine. We'd just have to wait – both of us.

Since I taught on Fridays from nine till four, with a meeting for lunch, there was little chance for me to repine. I managed to fit in a zap round Safeway's before choir practice in the evening, and then, having had the forethought to leave the car at home, I drank rather more wine than was sensible. Back home, I collapsed into what I hoped would be a deep and dreamless sleep. I could trust Andy not to wake me when he let himself in.

Chapter Four

I woke so suddenly that I didn't know where I was. What the hell—? Then came another scream, from my spare room. *Andy*!

I was in his room, switching on the light, before I realised I was on my feet.

'It's all right, love. It's only one of your dreams. Come on – wake up!' I sat on the bed, shaking him gently, as I'd done so often when we were children.

At last he woke. He grabbed me convulsively. 'Ruth?'

'No, love, it's me. Sophie. You've been having one of your nightmares. Wake up, now.'

He pulled himself into my arms; I pressed his head to my chest, as if we were six again. 'What was all that about?' But I knew, didn't I? 'How about a cup of tea?'

He was swinging himself out of bed before we realised he'd been sleeping in the nude.

'Hang on! I'll get you my dressing-gown.'

It was a unisex towelling affair, a little long for me, and he always used it when he came so he could travel light – an overnight case held all he needed. He was, however, the only visitor I had who always brought his own rubber gloves so he could wash up.

'Jesus,' he said, wrapping my dressing-gown round him.

'Tea? Or cocoa, or whiskey?' I asked. 'Here or downstairs?'

He shuddered. 'Cocoa. Downstairs. *Christ*!'

Fortunately I'd enough milk for cocoa, and I doubled his usual intake of sugar. And, on second thoughts, mine. His hands were still shaking when he wrapped them round the mug. It was his favourite, with a transfer of a Ferrari on the front; it reminded him of the shiny red one he'd written off fifteen years ago.

'You'd better tell me all about it,' I said, sitting next to him at the kitchen table. 'I know something's up.'

'You always did.' He didn't move, though, still clutching the cocoa mug with both hands; the dressing-gown sleeves, far too short, rode up his forearms. 'You haven't got any of your home-made jam, have you?' He got up to rummage in the usual cupboard, but had to make a grab for decency. 'Tell you what, I'll go and put some knickers on and get you your duvet. That nightie looks horribly like winceyette but you'll still need something.'

'I dress for warmth and chastity these days,' I said, lightly.

The clocks on the cooker, the microwave and the ghetto-blaster told me it was four-twenty-three. Good job it was Saturday – I had a terrible feeling I wasn't going to get much sleep this particular night. I switched on the central heating: we might as well be miserable in comfort. Then I made thick toast, found the jam. I reached out honey too, just in case.

He came back, wearing remarkably cheery striped socks, and thrust a similar pair at me: I put them on, and wrapped myself in the duvet he'd brought down. Then he produced an envelope from the dressing-gown pocket and spread in front of me a set of colour photos. I rubbed the last of the bleariness from my eyes and looked. Andy's BMW, with a scar on the bonnet as if a child had scribbled on a black-board; Ruth's new Mercedes, open-top and in the sky-blue of a Corgi model, with a spray of white lilies on its bonnet. Not at all cheery.

'That's what worries me,' he said, pointing at the funeral flowers.

'The whole thing worries me,' I said. 'Have you read any newspapers recently?'

He counted them off on his fingers, as if humouring me: the *Guardian, Irish Times, Independent*.

'Not the *Evening Mail*?'

He looked at me sharply. 'OK – tell me.'

I told him.

We sat in silence, our hands clasped. At last he pushed away, and sought the comfort of jam and butter, spreading them thickly on the toast. 'Fuck the diet,' he said, as if I'd protested.

'What have you done about this so far?' I asked. 'Apart from the police?'

'Not the police.'

'Not the – you're joking!'

'Private investigator. I want it all kept confidential.'

'You must be off your head!'

He looked away, irritated. Then he turned back. 'I want to do this job for UNICEF more than I've ever wanted anything in my life. It's important. I want to do it now, while the punters remember me, and I don't want anything to stop me. *Anything.*' He pushed himself to his feet and stalked to the far end of the kitchen, forgetting that it's hard to look dignified in an undersized towelling bath-robe. Especially when you're wearing stripey socks.

My desire to laugh was extinguished by what I had to say. 'There's one thing'll stop you. And that's what this lot is threatening you with.'

'There's a bodyguard with me all the time.'

I searched ostentatiously under the table.

'In an Espace, parked outside. Tailed my taxi from the airport. And I'll be safe enough at the Music Centre – the roadies have all toured with me for years.'

'What about the local team?'

'They'll only be using people I've worked with before.'

I raised an eyebrow. 'With all the activity erecting the set, Attila the Hun could get in and no one'd notice.'

'Passes.'

'Passes, schmasses. You can't tell me all those odds and sods who float around have passes.'

'They do this time. Special liggers' passes. Actually says "ligger" on it. And,' he added triumphantly, 'it's not just a pass they need, but the right colour cord round their neck.'

'Ligatures,' I said, grimacing at my own pun.

'Different colour neck-cords for each type of pass, the

colour combination known only on the day and decided at random.'

I wrinkled my nose. A statistic about the number of murder victims who knew and trusted their murderers was niggling somewhere in the recesses of my mind.

'Still think you ought to tell the police. Chris, for instance – he'd know what to do.'

'It's not unknown,' he said, 'for people under police protection to be attacked. Is it?'

'Point taken. All the same—'

'Tell you what, we'll argue about it in the morning. Night, love.' He kissed me absently on the cheek and went back to bed.

I met him again an hour later, trying to sneak downstairs without waking me. At the time I was trying to sneak downstairs without waking him. We plodded in silence back to the kitchen.

'What do you do when you can't sleep?' he asked.

'Clean out a drawer,' I said.

'What?' His face was so appalled it was comical.

'Clean out a drawer. There was this man at college had the most appalling insomnia – tried everything the National Health could suggest and then some. Anyway, he fetched up with a hypnotherapist, expecting a swinging watch before the eyes. But he didn't get it. He got forty quids' worth of advice, though. The therapist asked what he hated most. Cleaning the kitchen floor, he said. Right, said the therapist, that's what you'll do tonight when you can't sleep. And tomorrow. And the night after. Carl couldn't believe his ears. I usually have a milky drink and read, he said. Quite, said the therapist. And you don't sleep. You're rewarding yourself for not sleeping. This way you'll sleep. It may take a week, if you're a slow learner.'

Andy was grinning at last. 'How long did it take?'

'Three nights. Now, I don't mind kitchen floors, but I hate drawers.'

'Better fetch my rubber gloves,' he said, emptying the cutlery drawer into the sink.

'I can't think,' I said, greeting him at eleven with a light kiss, 'of a nicer way to be woken than by the smell of bacon.'

He raised a disbelieving eyebrow.

'OK. Not many nicer ways.' Chris believed in alarm clocks, and early-morning exercises. He considered sex something you did before you went to sleep, and when I'd once tried to alleviate some dawn boredom he'd had a tantrum but no erection. I sighed at the memory.

Not too surprisingly, Andy made the connection. 'Is Chris coming to the gig? You'd rather he didn't? Think he'd disapprove?'

Chris and Andy had never met face to face. They'd spoken on the phone a couple of times, when Chris had happened to answer it for me, but neither had seemed particularly keen to take things further. Andy had heard a lot about Chris, however, seeming to have an uncanny knack of phoning whenever the offs of our relationship outweighed the ons.

'I don't know is the answer. To all of your questions. He's safely at Bramshill at the moment, busily male-bonding. Poor chap,' I added, 'he must hate it. He's distinctly unclubbable.'

'Drop him. Come on, you're how old?'

'Nine months older than you, pillock!'

'Thirty-six. I'd have thought your biological clock was ticking quite loudly by now. Aren't you leaving it a bit late?'

'For children, you mean? Lots of women leave it later than this.'

'You're not lots of women.'

I waited while he turned the bacon – apparently he was out of vegetarian mode already – and broke an egg into the frying pan. 'I know. And I don't seem to have the instincts of lots of women. OK, there was a bad year when I was about thirty, when I'd have loved a baby. But these days it just doesn't seem to worry me. All those students I teach – perhaps it's sublimation,' I added, not altogether joking.

'It's not just kids, though,' he said, 'Ruth and I – we can't. Nor the sex. It's the cuddle in the middle of the night, the person next to you that you can reach out and touch.'

It was having someone to hold when you had a nightmare.

Ruth.

I dug in the fridge for the bread.

'The trouble is,' he said, flipping the egg on to a plate and breaking another one into the pan, 'that being in a second-best relationship can stop you getting into the right one.'

'There isn't a right one on the horizon at the moment,' I said, angry that I was letting the bleakness show. 'And I have a penchant as great as yours for falling for the wrong person. At least Chris keeps me on the straight and narrow.'

'In that case you definitely ought to drop him. Tell you what – come down to Devon at Easter. I'll parade all the eligible young men I know before you.'

'Knowing your friends,' I said, 'that'll take all of two minutes.'

Chapter Five

'I can see why you need an ego-mobile,' I said, pulling into the artists' car park at the Music Centre and slipping the Renault in a space from which it could gaze in admiration at the row of six forty-ton articulated trucks. It must be a big set: though I knew other halls, like the National Exhibition Centre, could take up to thirty trucks' worth of gear. 'Something this size would get an inferiority complex if it had to do this very often.'

'Even the BMW looks pretty small by comparison. I hate to admit this, but I have been known to turn up in a Roller, on grounds of size alone. A full-size one.'

A man who could only be a minder had materialised from the Espace and was looking macho by Andy's door. He snatched it open, holding it while Andy got out, and gazing menacingly into the middle distance. I got out my side; I knew he wasn't paid to extend the same courtesy to me.

'What d'you mean, a full-size one?' I repeated. 'Aren't all Rolls Royces the same size?'

The minder cracked his face for a second as he slammed the car door.

'Tell the lady, Griff.'

I fished my bag from behind my seat, shut my door and zapped the central locking. Then, as all three of us fell into step, I prompted him: 'Yes, tell the lady.'

'There is this individual, miss—'

'Sophie, please!'

' – Sophie – for whom I once had the honour of working, who was what our politically-correct brethren might call vertically challenged. Being a professional, miss, you'll forgive me if I decline to reveal his identity: suffice to say he does not hail from this side of the Atlantic. This – individual – wanted to enhance his height, and after due consultation with his image-builders and agent hit on the obvious solution – he would be surrounded by things and people smaller than himself. None of his backing musicians or singers is more than five foot four tall. Nothing on the set is more than seventy-five per cent of its usual size.'

'You mean, drums and guitars and everything?'

'*Everything*. And when the gentlemen travels in his Rolls or limo, it is a scaled-down version of the market model. Three-quarter size. Built by hand.'

A look at his face told me he wasn't joking.

'And there was that fat guy you worked for, Griff – surrounded himself with overweight singers and dancers,' Andy said.

'And you – what tricks does Andy use, Griff?'

He shook his head.

I stopped dead. 'There *is* something, isn't there?'

'OK, OK,' Andy said. 'Doesn't matter if you know, after all. We have to be careful what colour spot they use, or my hair appears to go green. Not so bad now Ruth's found me something else to use.'

I looked at him sideways. 'I'll bet you wouldn't want that lot to find out, all the same.'

A knot of young women of all ages had gathered the far side of the artists-only gate. One was screaming, but most were simply calling Andy by name, and waving in friendly rather than frantic fashion. A couple of middle-aged security guards were adamant but not unpleasant about keeping the gate locked.

'Duty calls,' said Andy. 'You stay here with Sophie, Griff.' He dug in the inside pocket of his jacket and fished out a plastic ballpoint pen. Then he sauntered over, grinning as if they were long-lost cousins. But not quite how he grinned at me.

'Wish he wouldn't bloody do this,' said Griff.

'You've tried stopping him?'

'Have you ever tried to stop him doing anything he wanted to do?'

'Trying to make him do something he doesn't want to do isn't easy, either. Which force were you with?'

'The Met. At least he's not insisting on having the gate opened,' he added. 'Got more sense now he's married to Miss Jean Groupie.'

I didn't think Ruth deserved that, and said so.

'No offence meant. We all got our names. And if you've ever worked in a set-up like this, you'll know we call spades fucking shovels.'

I nodded: the average roadie wasn't into self-restraint when it came to verbal exchanges.

Andy was walking back at last, unhurried despite the wind. He turned and waved; the women waved back with enthusiasm.

Despite the passes and the neck-cord, which was blue and white and bore the unlikely legend 'Baggies Bounce Back' – Andy being a determined West Bromwich Albion supporter – we were stopped at the door. Andy hesitated a microsecond until he was recognised; Griff followed as if glued to his shoulder. I tried to, but was intercepted.

'Come on, young lady, you know you can't come in here.'

I brandished my pass.

'They all try that. Not hard to get hold of one from somewhere.'

'This one got hold of hers from Rivers himself,' said Griff.

'The fucking Money?'

'The same,' he said darkly, 'and I don't doubt he'd welcome a bit of respect.' He grabbed my arm and propelled me along faster than my legs were designed to go until we caught up with Andy outside his dressing room. Clearly someone with a sense of humour had been giving thought to protecting him: he was installed in the room set aside for the Midshires Symphony Orchestra's Chief Conductor, Peter Rollinson. It was heavily personalised by its rightful tenant: framed cartoons on the walls; family photos on the desk; shelves filled with books. Being there at all felt like trespassing. No, Andy wouldn't mind giving this up.

Griff, square-shouldered and officious, elbowed into the

bathroom; you could almost see him reaching for a handgun, ready to react. But this time he returned with a palpable smile. 'Thought these classical types were supposed to be into austerity and things of the mind and that!'

Andy shrugged. He liked to blur distinctions, if possible – apart from his ethnic explorations he had worked with the Brodsky and the Duke Quartets. But he decided to indulge Griff and I followed him in. Apart from the usual shower, loo, etc, there was a big cornerways bath, complete with a family of yellow plastic ducks. But Andy's smile was pallid.

We trailed back to the sitting room. Despite the personal items it was curiously depressing; the calming shades of grey and green had badly misfired. And the atmosphere seemed to be rubbing off on its temporary occupant. What it needed was perking up. Andy's dressing rooms were usually lush with flowers, weren't they?

'No roses?' I asked.

'At this time of year, where do roses come from? Roses come from Africa. Are roses indigenous to Africa? No, roses are not indigenous to Africa. So if you want to grow roses in Africa you erect acres of greenhouses and divert millions of gallons of precious water from people who need it for their subsistence crops, then use more of the earth's precious resources flying the roses to European markets.'

'OK. No roses. Not so much as a British daffodil?'

'Wouldn't mind some of those,' he said. 'But they're not a priority. Ah, Jonty!'

Jonty, the tour manager he'd worked with for years, gave me a smacking kiss and his watch an anxious glance. 'There've been a couple of glitches,' he said. 'Tobe's left the sodding sound system boot-up disks at the Mondiale – didn't find out till five minutes ago, stupid bastard. I've sent a local gofer to pick them up.' He made it sound as if the guy would have to travel miles rather than a couple of hundred yards up the road; Griff caught my eye. 'And there's been a couple of the Brummie roadies sacked. Don't know the meaning of "no drugs tour". So what I thought we'd do is . . .'

Raising a hand to Griff, I drifted off. It'd be nice to organise some daffodils for Andy, to try and lift the gloom that had descended on him, though I was reluctant to go out myself only to have to confront the Cerberus who'd questioned my ID on the way back. No doubt Ollie would know a gofer who'd got a couple of minutes to spare. If there was any work still to be done it was probably in the capable hands of the touring roadies; the Brummies would have done their whack.

The place was alive with Wind of Change T-shirts and sweat-shirts. There was no Ollie to be seen backstage; I'd go round the front. Perhaps, though, I'd better look in on Karen first, to see how she was getting on.

There was a cheerful babble coming from the group of women washing up. It looked as if they were just coming to the tail-end of the lunch-time crockery: there were far more clean plates than dirty stacked on caterers' trolleys. Despite my late breakfast I helped myself to a couple of prawny pastries, which proved to be more-ish but unfilling, and sang out a greeting to Jill, Ollie's wife and supposedly Karen's mentor. Of Karen herself there was no sign. If the wretched girl had let Jill down . . .

Jill stripped off her rubber gloves and hugged me. 'Your little friend's made a great hit,' she said, surveying the work that was left.

'Does that mean she's not pulling her weight?'

'Well, it's her first time. Stars in her eyes.'

'Stars my arse. She's paid fifty quid to help!'

'She did quite well on the breakfast stint. Then Ollie decided to show her around – you know what an old softie he is. Funny, the thing that impressed her the most was the catering team. Or, at least, one of the guys in it. I must admit he's gorgeous – legs that go on forever and the neatest little bum.'

'Show me!'

'Into cradle-snatching, are you?'

'It's called having a toy boy. And I could use one.' I thought briefly of Chris – even more briefly of Carl, who still carried a torch for me – and sighed. 'Yes, I could certainly use one,' I repeated.

'There's always Phiz!' Jill crammed a couple of vol-au-vents into her mouth, resumed her gloves, and picked up a pile of plates. 'You know he's panting for you.'

'He's panting for anything in a skirt. I meant to warn Karen—'

'I think young Peachy Bum has put paid to any chances Phiz might have had. Go on, go and have a look.'

'See you later then!'

Armed with a chicken leg, neatly boned and stuffed with something interesting, I toddled off to the kitchen. Sure enough, there was Karen, poring over tarot cards and swigging a bilious-looking brew from a pint glass. She turned another card, and absently poured another slurp of liquid from the juicer goblet.

'What the hell d'you think you're doing? And where the hell is Sam?'

Sam was Andy's chef, ready to indulge whatever diet Andy happened to be following at the time. When he was in junk carnivore mode, Sam's burgers were magic – but should his employer enter a more self-denying phase, Sam was ready with lentils. He'd probably have worked wonders with stewed hair-shirt, if called upon.

'Keep your wool on, woman! Hey, it's Sophie – how are you, our kid?'

'G'day, Sam!' My Aussie accent was no more convincing than his Black Country one.

Karen shuffled, leaning forward on the table to give him the benefit of her bosom, which owed something, but not everything, to a Wonderbra and a low-cut T-shirt. Someone should have told her that she was wasting her time, but I figured she was safer trying to persuade him of the advantages of heterosexual behaviour than trying a similar line with Phiz. As if he'd been doing it all along, Sam started juicing items from a eclectic assortment of fruit and vegetables; the resultant liquid would go into one of the flasks Andy took on stage with him for between-number swigs. One of the guitar technicians swapped flasks as they were emptied. There would also be bottles of mineral water; like the Queen, Andy had Malvern water wherever he went.

I realised I couldn't start yelling about lack of security when no one but me knew why Andy's people should be especially vigilant. 'Hey,' I began, 'what's this Jill was saying about a gorgeous young man with legs up to his armpits?'

'Where? I'll fight you for him! Oh, you mean young Tony. Frightfully straight, luvvie. No good to me at all. And, though I die to say it, a bit on the young side for you. He might do for young Karen here – and of course, they have an immense bond already. They both come from Acocks Green, save the mark.'

Karen withdrew her bosom and pouted, not very effectively.

'Enjoying yourself?' I asked her. 'Good. Now, Andy usually goes and says hello to people as he makes his way to the stage – they'll be giving the lighting and sound one last check about two-thirty, I should think. So you'd better pop off and look busy.'

She took it for what it was – a rebuke – and flounced off.

' "Exit, pursued by a bear." You were a bit grumpy with her, sweetie.'

'She brings it out in me. Like a rash. And she is supposed to be working, not having her fortune told.' I looked at the tarot cards still stacked beside the juicer. 'Is she going to marry a tall, dark, handsome stranger?'

Sam shoved the cards in his back pocket and unpeeled a banana. 'You know I never, ever reveal the secrets of the cards.' To my mind he sounded more guilty than offended. 'Look, Sophie, Andy's due on stage for the sound-check in ten minutes, and this stuff won't juice itself.'

I took myself off. By now Ollie might well be in the auditorium, so I sauntered up on to the stage, into the organised chaos that always precedes a major gig. Six articulated lorries hold a great deal, and there was an army of men to deal with it. Mob-handed, that was how Jonty described it.

I heard Jonty and Ollie before I saw them.

'What d'you mean, he can't get the fucking things? There's no fucking sound without the disks!'

'The fuzz have sealed it off. The whole suite. Searching it. A tip-off.'

I'd never seen Jonty have a tantrum before. If asked, I'd have put money on his remaining cool in the face of the four-minute warning; but he was practically in tears, and his language got proportionately more lurid.

Ollie took it for a bit, then cracked. 'Jesus, you're just full of shit – you know that?'

'OK.' The voice was Andy's. 'What's up? Jonty?'

'I told you Tobe had left the disks back at the Mondiale? Well, Ollie's man went to get them and isn't back yet. Says the fuzz have sealed your suite.'

'No point you two yelling at each other,' said Andy. 'What's this about the police?' His voice lost its admonitory edge.

'A tip-off. Drugs.'

'*Drugs!* What the hell – anyone seen Sophie?'

This was clearly my cue. 'Did I hear someone take my name in vain?'

'You know a load of policemen. Get on the blower and find out what's going on. Someone's searching my hotel room for *drugs*, for Christ's sake!'

I shook my head. 'Chris isn't in that area. And the only other person I know with any clout is in Fraud. Jonty, you could phone the Drugs Squad and ask them to release the disks – put on your best Sandhurst accent and they'll eat out of your hand. And sort the rest out later.' I looked hard at Andy; he raised an eyebrow in return. A possible skirmish in the campaign against him: the possibility had to be considered.

Jonty reached for his mobile phone, turned his back on us and started talking. He paced backwards and forwards, gesturing with frustration.

Andy turned towards me, putting paid to any further contributions from Ollie. 'That kid – the student of yours – didn't she want a photo or something?'

'Didn't she introduce herself? I got her into the washing-up team.'

'Only saw the usuals.'

'Shit. If I can find her, have you got time now? I suppose you'll be running behind schedule.'

He grinned. 'It should all run like clockwork. Damn it, this is the thirtieth time we've done it! The set was up in record time. What d'you think of it?'

'Impressive. That big ramp projecting into the auditorium – is that where you strut your stuff and look sexy?'

'Believe me, all I think about is all I think about those people putting their lovely lucre into my trust fund. I codpiece for Africa, girl, and don't you forget it. Any luck, Jonty?'

'Plenty. And some of it good. The guy's on his way with the disks, so we shall have sound after all. And your suite is clean. Not surprising, since apparently you're not using it.' Jonty looked at me curiously.

'They can check the luggage in the artic. And my overnight case, which is still in Sophie's spare room. Didn't you tell them about it being a no-drugs tour?'

'I don't think believing people is a police attribute,' I said mildly. 'Anyway, how about that photo of you and Karen? Shall I fetch her?'

He took longer than I expected to make what I'd have thought was a minor decision. 'No, I'll walk round with you. You could bring her back up front – she could sit and watch. Remind her about no photos while we're working, though.'

I nodded. There'd be flashbulbs aplenty during the show, but Andy was superstitious about them beforehand.

I found Karen in the ladies' loo, her face puffy with tears. She'd popped in earlier, just to make sure she looked gorgeous for Andy, and had spent so long titivating that she'd missed his visit to the washers-up. There was another paroxysm of tears as she recounted her tale of woe.

'Come on, love – he's in his room waiting to meet you.'

'Not like this!'

I could see her point. Ironically, he'd have been at his best if she'd confronted him complete with tear-stains; he had one of the best hugs I'd ever been engulfed in.

'We'll have to do it later,' I said. 'I'll talk to Andy.' I couldn't promise anything; it wasn't my time I was disposing of.

By the time I reached Andy's dressing room, the door was locked. A post-it told me the disks had turned up and they were starting the run-through any moment now. I shrugged: no daffodils, and no photocall for Karen. At least she might look civilised enough by now to go front of house. Perhaps I was an old softie too.

There were several band wives sitting in the first three or four rows: I passed Karen a spare pair of ear plugs and settled down next to her in the near darkness. Someone on the lighting gantry at the back of the stage was having trouble with one of the spotlights, and the exchanges between the stage manager and the lighting engineer were so fruity that I glanced at Karen. However much of a Rivers fan her mother might be, she presumably wouldn't want her daughter to hear the F and C words used quite so prolifically – and, indeed, inventively. The trouble appeared to be that the huge Wind of Change Tour symbols intruded between Andy and the spot when he moved downstage; although the roadie who'd hung them insisted they were located in the precise position he'd used in Dublin, there was clearly a problem. Andy prowled restlessly about the stage, as if looking for something valuable. From time to time he glanced at his watch. He'd said very little about giving up music that wasn't positive; when I'd tried to talk about what he'd miss he'd been evasive. But giving the last performance for some time – possibly for ever, if he stuck to his resolution – must be a nerve-racking affair, especially on home territory. Everyone expected so much of him. And it wasn't just *his* last gig – it was the roadies', too. They would be out of work – as would the caterers and the PR team. OK, the good ones would drop into jobs with no difficulty – but times were hard for the average ones. As they were for us all.

At last everything seemed to be fixed. The lights for the first number came up: blackness at the rear of the set, and a cascade of bright lights like a curtain. The loudspeakers roared into action. Andy ran forward, as if breasting a waterfall.

And into the pool of light came the shape of a man, diving, diving towards him. He missed him by perhaps six inches.

Chapter Six

'Andy!' I was on my feet, scrambling over the barriers. 'Andy!' A jump and a heave, and I was on the stage.

Andy had staggered backwards but was now upright. The other man—

'Get the paramedics!' Was that my voice?

The music faltered to silence: the musicians on stage first, then, finally, the computerised system. Yes: it was my voice. And now it was joined by others. 'Paramedics! Quick, for Christ's sake!'

But from the angle of the man's body, from the blood trickling from nose, mouth and ears, I didn't think there was much they could do. I could hear slow feet: a St John's volunteer. I wanted the paramedics that were part of Andy's entourage, travelling everywhere with him just in case. 'No! You look after them.' I pointed to the women I'd left. 'Ollie – call an ambulance!' I yelled. I tore off my jacket and laid it pointlessly over the man's torso; Andy took a second to realise what I was doing, and started to strip his, but he was beginning to shake. He'd missed death himself by inches.

'Sophie?' His hand reached for mine.

I sat him down on a convenient ramp, and realised I was trembling too.

Someone had the sense to turn on all the working lights and douse the spots. The band and backing singers formed a horrified circle. Pete. Pete Hughes: that was the name going round. At last two paramedics arrived; they took one look and shooed us away.

I had to get Andy back to the safety of his room. Somewhere in the row of onlookers might be the injured roadie's partner. And then there was Karen—

'Ollie?'

He stepped forward.

'Ollie – can you organise Karen and the others backstage? Tea, coffee? Griff – get Andy back to his room. Don't let anyone in.' I sounded calm – quite authoritative, in fact. I tried not to look at what the paramedics were doing. When one of them broke off for a moment, I said, 'If there's even a whisper of hope, get a helicopter to transport him. Andy'll pay.'

He shook his head. 'Probably better to get the fuzz to close off road junctions. Not all that far to City Hospital.'

'Do what's best,' I said. 'But if you need a chopper—'

The ambulance men – also paramedics, according to their uniform – took years to come: five-and-a-half minutes by my watch. By then Jonty was with me on the stage, together with several security men in the Music Centre uniform.

'The police'll be on their way, Jonty,' I said.

There was a murmur from the handful of roadies still on stage.

'Automatic, with an accident like this,' I said.

'Won't be popular,' he said. 'It's a self-regulating world. Don't want the Bill poking their noses in.'

'Tough. It's a no-drugs tour, isn't it – that's one thing you don't have to worry about.'

'Don't you believe it. The contents of Birmingham's sewage system won't bear analysis in about three minutes from now. And sometimes there's one or two bits of half-inching, too. Nothing major,' he added hastily, 'we all know each other too well. Don't rob your mates, do you?' He rubbed his hands across his face, suddenly older than his forty years. What a way to end his career with Andy. 'Better call the Health and Safety people,' he added. 'Injury at work. Hope to Christ Ollie insisted on everyone wearing full safety harness.'

I nodded, hardly listening; something else had occurred to me. 'Jonty – tell the Music Centre people not to let anyone out. Or in, for that matter.'

He looked at me quizzically. Hadn't Andy confided in him?

'There's just a chance,' I said, 'that someone could have seen something but not want to get involved. You know how it is.'

The ambulancemen started to move what was left of Pete. One or two of the roadies crossed themselves as they passed.

A tour paramedic stood up, stripping his gloves. He came over to me. 'They're clearing Dudley Road to give us a through run. But he'll never make it.'

I shook my head: there was nothing to say. And then I remembered my jacket. That bloody mess of rag. 'I'm sorry. In the pocket.' I pointed. 'My keys—'

He slid his hand in, held out two bunches. 'You won't want your jacket, will you, miss.'

'Andy, you have to tell the police now,' I said, making tea – there was a supply tucked discreetly beside a cupboard that turned out to be a fridge. I stirred in sugar and pushed the cup and saucer into his hands.

'It was an accident! The man was on a high gantry. You know how they forget about harnesses.'

I gave him the sort of look I usually reserve for thick students.

'Andy, listen. Someone has been telling you that they want you dead. The cars – the obituary – someone dies on your set—'

He put down the cup and saucer, dreadfully genteel, and walked to the window that overlooked the covered mall. Down there, the water clock told us that it was three-thirty. And for the first time I noticed that Pete Hughes's blood had spattered Andy's jeans.

'It was a fucking accident. What I have to do now is decide whether or not to go on with the show.'

There was a scratch at the door, and Jonty slipped in silently, as if in the presence of death. He made straight for the fridge and found a miniature whisky which he downed it as if it were cold tea. Then he looked more closely at Andy. 'One of these wouldn't do you any harm, either,' he said. 'And for Christ's sake get those bloody jeans off.' As he realised what he'd said he bolted for the bathroom.

I caught Andy's eye and nodded. 'Just step out of them. Where's your dressing-gown?'

'Over there.'

I threw it. 'As soon as Jonty's finished spewing I suggest you get in there too – shower, have a bath, whatever. Make you feel better. Then you can think about the gig.'

'Thought already,' he said, turning his back and slipping off his jeans. 'Got to go on, hasn't it? OK, the punters'll know there's been an accident, and there won't be a more subdued bunch of roadies in the western hemisphere, but the trust's been promised its share of the takings, and that guy's family can have my own share. Scrub the party afterwards. The food can be given to the homeless.'

'Better phone Ruth, in case the media pick up anything and exaggerate it.' His mobile phone was on the table near me: I tossed it over and pointed to the dressing room. 'It's more private in there.'

But he tapped the number where he was, peering like a fugitive between the grey vertical blinds at the mall and its water clock.

I busied myself with tea for Jonty, which he drank as tentatively as other people tackle neat whisky, told him what Andy had decided, and took myself off to check on Karen.

Whoever designed and equipped the Music Centre had a sense of social order that Mozart and Haydn would have recognised. Most of the Centre is luxurious: the auditorium itself is sumptuous in wood and plush. The backstage regions, however, have all the glamour of a public lavatory, elegance having been abandoned for functional concrete, metal stair-rails and cold blue paintwork – apart from the areas that international artists might be expected to see, of course. So the corridors and stairs Andy and his entourage trod were carpeted and well-lit: those frequented by the roadies and caterers were reminiscent of a run-down, thirties-built NHS hospital. There was an irrepressible rumour that the Music Centre management had tried to ban members of the Midshires Symphony Orchestra from public areas like bars while they were in their working clothes – their working clothes being evening suits and long black dresses. I wondered what the management made of the jeans-and-trainers uniform of Andy's crew.

After the cups of tea, there was a lot of washing up, and I rather hoped to find Karen remembering her obligations. Jill was busy, and the other women – but not Karen. Cursing under my breath, and possibly out loud, I went to find the caterers.

I found a rebellion.

Sam explained: Jonty had said probably no party. OK, they could quite see why not. But what was this about everyone having to hang about in this benighted dump when there was enough time to see a little of Birmingham? If indeed, as he personally doubted, there was anything of Birmingham worth seeing. I shrugged, and muttered something non-committal about the police.

'Jonty says that was your idea. Jesus, calling the bloody cops!'

I wondered briefly whether to trust him, but decided against it. 'My boyfriend—' I stopped. I loathed the term. But surely Sam wouldn't be politically correct enough to demand the word companion, and whatever else Chris was he certainly wasn't my partner. 'My boyfriend's in the police. The routine rubs off. Probably the fuzz themselves will tell you all you can go.'

'I wish.' He stared malevolently at the empty juicer. 'I wonder what flavour His Nibs'll want tonight.' He juggled a couple of mangoes.

'Phone and find out,' I said briefly. 'Seen Karen anywhere?'

'I told her big bad Auntie Sophie would be after her, so she's washing up, isn't she?'

'Not so as you'd notice. Seen young Peachy Bum anywhere? She could be seeking consolation in his arms.'

'He's in the First Aid Room – fainted clean away when he heard what had happened. Any news, by the way?' All the camp frivolity left his voice.

I shook my head. 'And I can't imagine that it'll be good

when we get it. Poor bugger. Any theories floating around about how it might have happened?'

'Plenty. And all contradictory. Why don't you go and have a nose round? You're Family, after all. You're entitled.' He picked up a melon; the conversation was at an end.

That was exactly what I wanted to do; but there was still the small matter of Karen. Not expecting miracles, I looked back at the washer-uppers – and, to my amazement, there she was, wielding a tea towel as if she'd never done anything else. I would leave well alone.

As I headed up the steps to the stage I was intercepted by a policewoman. 'Excuse me, miss, you can't go up there at the moment – the Health and Safety people are busy. Authorised personnel only.'

I flapped my pass at her – the one that gave me access to everywhere except the Pyrotechnics Room. She looked impressed, and waved me through.

There wasn't much to see; it had the desolate air I associate with a room after a party. A middle-aged woman wearing a hard hat was scaling the lighting gantry; a young man was busy with a tape measure and calculator. A police sergeant watched them with a preoccupied air, but looked round quickly enough when I appeared.

'I'm Sophie Rivers,' I said. 'Andy just wondered—'

'Not a lot I can tell you,' he said. 'Except they don't seem to have found anything wrong with the guy's safety harness clips, or the clip points.'

'So—?'

'So they'll no doubt let the management know their findings as soon as they're ready, Mrs Rivers. If you'll tell your husband that.'

Somewhere on my back I took a wrong turning and found myself looping round the deserted building. The acoustic rooms, the practice rooms, they all echoed with the question: who wanted Andy dead? And another question, pounding with each step I took: why, why, why?

Eventually I made my way back to Andy. Griff, stern and

alert, stood outside his door, with another, younger, bullet-headed man.

''Ave to search you, sweetie.'

'Stow it. This is Ms Rivers—'

'The Money's missus?'

'Cousin. Not that we don't show any woman we come into contact with absolute respect.' His new colleague looked doubtful. 'But she's the only one we let in without checking first with Andy – who, by the way, is Mr Rivers to you, and never the Money in front of anyone. *Ever*. And she's the only one we leave alone with him.'

'What about Mrs M—'

'It's Mrs Rivers, and she's not here. OK?'

The bruiser nodded sullenly.

I smiled at Griff. 'You'd have made a splendid infants' teacher.'

'I'm a killer on the PTA,' he said, straight-faced. 'Better go on in, Sophie. He's got company, by the way.'

'Company' turned out to be a couple of uniformed officers, trying to piece together what had happened. I gave them my story.

'Come on, miss – you must have seen more than that.' The constable tried to look stern, but since he was scarcely old enough to shave he wasn't very convincing.

'When you've got all those loudspeakers going at full belt, when the lights are specifically angled to prevent you seeing anyone except Andy, you can't tell what's going on,' I said. 'I'm sure someone will demonstrate – Jonty would fix it.'

Jonty nodded.

'Might be useful,' conceded the elder officer, a ginger-haired woman sergeant of about my age: Kerry, Andy soon discovered, was her first name, but I don't think he troubled about her surname.

'What about the show?' Andy asked. 'I want it to go ahead. *Everyone* wants it to go ahead. Do we have to get permission, Kerry?'

'From the Health and Safety Inspectors, sir,' she said. No doubt to her acute embarrassment, a vivid blush oozed up her neck, until her whole face was awash.

'If the show were to go ahead, would you both like

tickets?' Women have gone down on their knees for a smile like that: to do Andy justice, I don't think he meant it to be as devastating as it always was. 'Could you see to it, Jonty?'

If I knew anything about it, they'd come. And Jonty would ensure they had some merchandise to take away at the end of the evening. It wasn't bribery, just PR. It had worked on Lady Thatcher, when she was plain Mrs T, though Andy would never reveal even to me the size of the personal donation she made. Yes, given a chance, he'd charm money for UNICEF out of the most red-necked, jingoistic American senator. Given a chance.

'You have to tell them. There may be something there on that stage that'll help trace whoever it is that's threatening you. Can't you get that into your head? More to the point, there may be something there that'll help the police find out what happened to Pete. If the police treat it as a straight accident, they'll give no more than a cursory inspection to the stage. They may miss something vital.'

'The Health and Safety people said—'

'They said they found no problems with any equipment. They didn't look for anything else. Why would they? They've no reason to be suspicious.'

He was silent.

'What did Ruth say?'

He looked me straight in the eye. 'Find who did it,' he said. 'And have the party. Call it a wake.'

The sergeant, her skin icing-pale again, was clearly out of her depth. Quite clearly she wanted to yell at him for his foolhardiness: equally clearly she was too much in awe of him to do anything of the sort.

The woman she summoned – acting Detective Inspector Stephenson – had no such qualms. She turned up within fifteen minutes of the sergeant's call. One step behind her was another plain-clothes officer, my old friend Ian Dale, who greeted everyone, including me, with exaggerated formality. When I caught his eye he raised an eyebrow by a millimetre, enough to hint at his acute discomfort. DI

Stephenson was a well turned out woman. Her make-up and hair were immaculate; her trousers were a make I'd rejected as too expensive even half-price in the sale. And they looked better on her than they ever would have on me, since she was about five-foot ten in her socks.

'Right,' she said, 'get all these people out of here, will you, Sergeant? I want to talk to Mr Rivers.'

Chapter Seven

'Everyone's been reshuffled,' Ian said. 'And I can't wait till I'm old enough to retire.' He leaned against the corridor wall outside Andy's room.

He'd ushered us all out, though Andy plainly wanted me to stay, and he was supposed to be going back in to support the inspector. But he was clearly in no rush. His face was longer, more lugubrious and Eyoreish than ever: even the leather patches on his elbows were coming unstitched.

'When'll Chris be back from Bramshill?' I asked. 'Not long, now, surely?'

'Another couple of weeks,' said Ian, ignoring the clear implication that Chris and I must be in one of our off-periods. 'And they'll be after chaining him to a desk. Not supposed to run around getting their hands dirty any more, these Senior Officers.' He snorted over the capital letters.

I tutted. From within the room a voice summoned him; he raised depressed eyebrows, shrugged, and turned away.

'I ought to be in there with him,' I said. 'Andy. He's my cousin.'

'I remember,' he said, with forbearance. 'I'll see what I can do.' He patted me on the shoulder and went on, closing the door firmly behind him.

I found myself dabbing my eyes: shock, I suppose. Griff and the bouncer were a few yards down the corridor, talking vigorously with Kerry and her young constable; Ollie and the others were sorting out the stage for a makeshift rehearsal. One of the backing singers would walk through

Andy's actions. Ollie had agreed with Ruth: the party would go ahead, for the sake of everyone involved.

The door opened behind me. DI Stephenson was prepared to admit me to her presence, was she? I walked over to join Andy on the sofa, and then changed my mind; he was so pale I was afraid he might faint. Perhaps his blood sugar level was low after the shock. I went back to the door and summoned Griff.

'Go and get a couple of sandwiches, would you? There's a cafe in the mall. Film-wrapped ones. Salad or cheese – he's in vegetarian mode again.' Then I remembered the breakfast bacon, but it wasn't worth the complications of changing my mind.

'Not asking Sam to rustle something up, I notice.'

'He's busy juicing,' I said stupidly.

Griff held my gaze steadily for a moment. 'I think I take your meaning. And if I choose a couple of sarnies at random – and a couple for you, Sophie? – no one'll be any the wiser. Right?'

'Right.'

I wasn't quite sure what I meant; all I'd thought of was feeding Andy. But perhaps – no, I couldn't make sense of anything. I went back in, to DJ Stephenson's obvious irritation. I should have explained first; it wasn't like me to be as abrupt, as rude, as I'd obviously seemed. 'Sorry,' I said. 'I just thought Andy ought to eat.'

She gestured me down to the sofa. Andy took my hand. She stood over us, studying her note pad. 'Mr Rivers has had a number of implicit threats against his life. He tells me you are aware of another. Could you tell me in your own words, please?'

I explained about the newspaper death notice. 'If Andy hadn't been against publicity I'd have tried to trace the person who inserted it. The *Evening Mail* people have a system to guard against hoaxes.'

'I'm sure such investigations will be safe in our hands, thank you, Miss Rivers.'

I was aghast. All the police officers I'd ever met had been friendly and informal, using first names as soon as they could. Perhaps the word 'acting' in her title was making her insecure. But just at the moment I could have done without having to make allowances for other people's foibles.

Ian sighed, heavily.

'Thanks, Inspector,' I said, with no irony at all. 'Do you think this afternoon's incident might have a connection?'

Wrong again: I could see Ian tense. *Slow down, Sophie. Let the woman do her job her own way.* I smiled at her, placatingly. 'Sorry – I'm jumping the gun, rather, aren't I? Is there any other way I can help you?'

She'd probably have liked to tell me simply to shut up, but a knock at the door interrupted her: Griff and the sandwiches. He'd even cadged some plates to put them on when they were unwrapped.

Andy stared at me as if I were off my head. 'What about Sam? That's what he's here for.'

I shook my head; I didn't know either. Did Griff really think Sam was capable of poisoning Andy? He certainly seemed to think I might have the same suspicious. At last I asked a question I should have put an hour ago. 'What were you looking for on stage? While they were pithering with the spot?'

He looked blank.

'You were wandering about the stage looking as if you'd lost something. Peering round. Picking things up.'

'Oh! My flask! I'd forgotten. Pete . . .' He broke off, shuddering.

'I think Miss Rivers is right – you ought to eat something,' Inspector Stephenson said magnanimously. While he peeled the cellophane, she suddenly frowned. 'What flask?'

'I keep a flask of juice on stage. There's half a dozen kept in the wings, so when I finish one I can start another. One of the lads swops the empty one for a full one.'

'How many people know about the flasks?'

'All the roadies. All the punters, for that matter. I used to keep it out of sight, but now I always leave it front left. Singing's a thirsty business. You can quickly get dehydrated. No harm in everyone knowing that.'

'Juice?'

'Sam – he's my chef, tours everywhere with me – juices a variety of fruit and vegetables.'

'Anything else in there?' Her voice was still calm, but I had a nasty idea what she was getting at.

Andy stared at her.

'Such as – substances – to keep up your energy levels, Mr Rivers?'

He was on his feet before I could stop him. 'Absolutely not! Where have you been these last few years, woman?'

'All right, Andy, all right.' Ian, large and impregnable, was on his feet too. 'Andy's got quite a reputation for anti-drugs work, ma'am. Chris – DCI Groom, ma'am – was telling me Andy's been co-opted on to a Home Office working party. That's right, isn't it, Sophie? And he's done all those TV ads, of course.'

All those first names! Ian was making a point, wasn't he?

'And it's a no-drugs tour,' I added. 'In fact, weren't a couple of roadies sacked earlier today for violating the rule?'

'Are you alleging something, Miss Rivers?'

Was I? I shook my head. 'Just making a point about Andy's attitude to drugs.'

'Perhaps you should let him make his own points.'

It would be better to keep quiet and use the space to think. It didn't work, of course; I found my mind circling round the flask, which had of course occupied the same spot, front left, for all the rehearsals and performances I'd ever been to. It had become quite a feature: at the end of each performance Andy would lob an empty flask into the audience. So why hadn't it been there today? Nothing was ever out of place, whether the gig was in Newcastle or New York.

Time I ate too, perhaps. Griff had found a curious and expensive mixture of cheese, celery and mayonnaise, which didn't wholly fill the sandwich. Celery was supposed to clear the blood, wasn't it? I hoped it would clear my head.

Andy and Inspector Stephenson were maintaining a staccato conversation. When I looked up from my sandwich, Ian was staring at me with barely-hidden concern. I smiled; he raised his eyebrows as if to prompt me.

'Inspector Stephenson?' I'd interrupted her thought flow: too bad. 'Andy's tours are always meticulous down to the last detail. Everything is always placed exactly where it was in the previous performance, and exactly where it will be in the next one. If that flask was missing—'

She sighed, rather too audibly, as well she might. 'Go and find it, will you, Sergeant? Just to put everyone's mind at rest.'

He got up with alacrity, probably glad to have something useful to do. With luck, he would come back with it, safe in a polythene bag, in case it had any fingerprints on it.

'What I can't understand,' Inspector Stephenson was saying, 'is – if you believe these threats – why you're prepared to perform tonight. Why don't you cancel? You've got the excuse of that man Hughes's accident.'

'In the Third World,' said Andy wearily, 'a child dies almost every second of a preventable disease. If, by walking on that stage, I can save a few hundred by getting them inoculated, how can I not? And in the part of Africa where my Foundation is working, the life expectancy for the average male is no more than forty. OK, so my life might be cut a little short, if the worst comes to the very worst. So what?'

I pressed my knuckles to my mouth in an effort not to speak.

Stephenson seemed moved; she coughed. 'I'm sure it won't come to that. We'll increase security – check bags, that sort of thing. But resources are very limited, Mr Rivers – Andy—' His charm had evidently claimed another victim. 'Miss Rivers?'

'Sophie, please. What I can't understand is why all the business with Andy and Ruth's cars went no further. Why did they do no more than drop nasty big hints? If you've got the chance to put funeral flowers on one car, vandalise another, you'd presumably have the opportunity to tamper with either in a much more dangerous way.'

'Perhaps they wanted to lead up to tonight's performance – the grand finale?' Andy's smile was very bleak.

Stephenson was quick to pick up the idea. 'How about Dublin? Berlin? Any problems at all there?'

'I'd already increased my personal security – you've met John Griffiths, I think.'

'Briefly. I'd like to talk to him at greater length.'

'The vandalism – whatever you want to call it – stopped then. But Sophie spotted that obituary in the paper and was alarmed.'

'I'm not surprised – a most unpleasant prank at the very least. Hell! Excuse me.' She turned away to talk into her phone. After a while, as Andy had done, she moved to the window, overlooking the mall.

There was a sharp tap at the door – Jonty. He was pale, but the tight lips and blazing eyes suggested anger. 'I've just had a phone call from the Press Association. Would I like to confirm that you died this afternoon. Would I buggery, I said.'

'Rumours of my death are greatly exaggerated,' Andy said quietly. 'What about—'

'He's on a life-support system. They don't think he'll make it, but they want to contact next of kin before they . . . Organ transplants. Guy carried the card . . . Someone's told the press Andy's died,' he said to Stephenson, as she clipped her phone shut. 'Fortunately they checked first before issuing the story.'

'Bastards,' she said. 'Absolute fucking bastards.'

At this point Ian returned, jiggling the flask in a polythene bag. He caught the full force of the inspector's invective and blinked, without apparent approval, but she noted his care with the flask and smiled, her whole face lightening as she did so. She took it from him and, holding the cap through the polythene, unscrewed it and sniffed. Her nose wrinkled attractively, Andy grinned. But his expression changed rapidly when she held the flask out to him.

'What the hell's Sam put in there?'

I slid sideways to sniff too. I've never been very impressed with Andy's concoctions, but this one smelt downright peculiar.

Stephenson screwed the top back firmly. 'I think I'd like to have the contents of this examined, Mr Rivers. Just in case.' Her voice was cold and official once more.

'I'd be very grateful,' he said, smiling as if she were doing him a favour.

But this time her face didn't soften.

Chapter Eight

It was all over. The last rapturous yells, the last wild applause, the last blown kisses. The stewards had pulled in the last bucketful of money for Andy's Foundation – this time it would be shared, as he'd told the fans, with the injured roadie's family, so they'd been extra-generous with their donations.

'Birmingham, I love you!' Andy had called for the last time.

And for the last time the stage plunged into darkness around him.

The official fan club had booked one of the smaller Music Centre halls for the party, and had decorated it to look like a giant tent – as if Andy's connection with Africa were more in the nature of a safari than a life-saving commitment. When he and his party – including Ian and me – went in, it was pitch black. Then the lights blazed up and there, in the centre of the room, her mouth taped ostentatiously, was Ruth.

Andy ran to her. The room boomed with applause, cat-calls and cheers. When, clutching a glass of champagne, I eventually made my way over, she had discarded the blue sticking-plaster and was flourishing a note pad and thick pen. 'Drove up this afternoon,' she wrote. 'Heard the concert. Brilliant!'

He hugged her again.

'Roadie?' she wrote.

'Still alive. Just,' Ian said, clearly entranced.

It couldn't be by her looks: Ruth was no bimbo, and I

reckoned that anyone could have identified her as a teacher at a hundred paces. On the other hand, the obvious intelligence of her eyes made her attractive, and I'd always envied her long, elegant hands. She'd got a good figure too: worked with weights and cycled a lot down in Devon. Just now she was wearing jeans, like most of us, and a silk shirt which by its very lack of ostentation – and there were some very showy garments indeed there tonight – declared its exclusive origins. She tried not to take much money from Andy – she'd been earning about three times my salary anyway when she gave up her job as the head of a mega-comprehensive school. I suspect she'd been a very good head: Labour shadow cabinet parents had queued up to send their children there, and, if they'd had any sense, Tory ministers would have done the same. Now she was bringing her administrative skills to bear on the Foundation. She drew a respectable salary from it, largely so she could make it public knowledge and prevent whispers.

Everyone worked very hard to make the party go with a suitable bang. There was a corner set aside for the roadies' and musicians' children: a climbing frame, a net full of plastic balls for them to wriggle through, quantities of Lego and Duplo, and a lovely wooden train. There were even a couple of women – proper nannies, according to Jonty – to look after them, so the mothers could let their hair down. At first people were predictably subdued, but the crush, the lavish provision of food – there had been, so Sam said, two teams of caterers competing to demonstrate their supremacy – and copious quantities of booze had guaranteed that if things could warm up, they would. And they did.

Karen brought her mother over to say thank you. Mrs Harris was probably about seven or eight years older than me, putting her in her mid-forties. She had a white blouse that aspired very hard to be posh, with a lot of gold chains lurking in the frilly neckline. Her skirt was shorter than I'd have expected, but she had very good legs, although they might have been improved by the absence of her shoes, which were much too low cut at the front in relation to the height of the heels. The poor woman was blushing painfully, as if I were someone important; I could hardly hear her husky whisper.

'Does he know – you know – lots of other stars?'

'I suppose so. But he doesn't name-drop very much.'

'Would he know people like – like Cliff? Or BarryanRobinanMaurice?'

I couldn't work that out, so I was pleased to spot Andy in host mode. So Mrs Harris and daughter were photographed one on each side of him, his arms round their shoulders, as he gave each of them a professionally affectionate kiss.

Ian spent most of his time with Ruth, whom he plied with champagne as if it were medicinal. By the time he'd finished, her note pad was full of scribbled comments on brands of dry sherry. I fended off the attentions of Phiz, and instead had a quick flirt with Jess, the extremely handsome black drummer. I caught a whiff of Duck's breath before he found me. In fact, things were going so well I completely forgot to miss Chris.

Then I found Griff by my side, looking serious. I followed him out into the quiet of the mall.

'I want Andy out of here,' he said. 'Pete's died.'

I shook my head to commiserate. Then I looked at him. 'What's the connection?'

'They want to do a post mortem. There are symptoms that might suggest something other than an accident. Something to do with his pupil dilation. You know what that means, Sophie?'

'Drugs?'

'Right. Now, Pete was a good clean guy.'

'So where did he get the drugs? Hang on. Andy's flask goes walkabout; Pete dives off the gantry: Andy's flask is found, and the contents smell distinctly odd. Are you thinking what I'm thinking?'

'Let's just say I shall be very interested in the results of the PM on Pete and on the analysis of Andy's flask.'

'So will the police,' I said. 'So how do we protect Andy? Presuming that if the juice was spiked it was intended for Andy.'

'I think we have to assume it was. What I've been thinking

is this. They know where he lives in Devon. They may have twigged where he stays in Brum. I'd like to get him and Ruth off up north to a place run by a friend of mine. Like a safe house. Ruth's brought clothes and things for them both. I phoned her,' he added. 'And no, she didn't come up in her Merc. A friend of mine drives a tatty old Lada. Apparently.'

I found I was beginning to like Griff. Then I wasn't so sure.

'Just to make sure they get away clean and easy, like, I'd like you to drive Andy back to yours as usual. Only it won't be Andy, see – it'll be a look-alike. And you'll find your car inside the building – in the unloading bay. I just wanted to make sure no one got their grubby little fingers on it.'

'Who will the look-alike be . . . No! *No!* Don't even begin to contemplate it! Phiz does *not* share a car with Sophie. Still less does he occupy Sophie's spare room.'

'He does look remarkably like Andy – from the back at least,' Griff said mildly. 'No, Sophie, as it happens, it will be my good self. I've provided myself with a wig and sunglasses for just such an eventuality. And I have to inform you that I will sleep with my door shut, because I snore, and that I will be happy to prepare breakfast at whatever hour you choose.'

I grinned. 'God, it's after well after two now. How do we break up the party?'

'Jonty's job. Nothing for you to worry about. And I'll sort out Andy and Ruth. Their driver's police-trained, by the way.'

'I'll bet you are too. Would you like to drive tonight, Mr Rivers? Feel like a bit of slumming with your old cousin?'

'I thought you'd never ask.'

Since – ostensibly – I was taking Andy home, I could scarcely say goodbye to him and Ruth. But I wandered back in, not wanting them to think – I didn't know what. I felt totally exhausted. If I closed my eyes, I saw Pete Hughes' broken body; my ears were still ringing from the concert despite the earplugs. When I found Andy and Ruth, I managed to imply – I hope – that I was going to say my farewells and get back to them. 'See you later,' I said: that's what we say in Brum, even when we know full well we won't see someone for weeks, so I wasn't, strictly, lying.

Griff drove home swiftly, unostentatiously. When we got back he waved a laminated sheet of tablets in a bubble-pack at me: sleeping tablets. Homeopathic ones. I'd seen them in health-food shops but never thought of trying them. Better than cleaning any more of the kitchen, perhaps.

'Might as well get some kip, love,' he said. 'You look as if you could use it. Might even try a couple myself.' He popped a couple and chewed them and passed me the sheet.

'Why is it,' Griff began, tipping scrambled eggs on to toast, 'that you can spend half the night listening to the God-awful row Andy produces and hardly notice the noise, but when you get out into leafy suburbia, and it's all quiet and allegedly peaceful, you can't sleep for the yelping of some bloody dog fox? And the little bleeder switches your security lights on too – just to make sure. Here, try that for size.'

'Thanks.' The eggs were wondrously fluffy. 'Learn this in the Met, did you?'

'There are few things you don't learn in the Met. Hmm – a little light on the cayenne . . . Thing is, Sophie, my wife wouldn't recognise a frying pan if it jumped up and hit her. She was the woman for whom TV dinners and microwaves were invented.'

'What's she do?'

'She's a housewife. Raised the kids.' He sounded slightly shocked.

I *was* slightly shocked. I didn't know any housewives. Those of my friends who had had children had taken maternity leave, or at the very most career breaks. I wondered what it would be like to spend endless hours in the house. Never a dull moment when the kids were small – but surely when they were older, when they left home?

'What does she do now?'

He looked puzzled. 'Looks after me, of course. Apart from the cooking, that is.'

'And?'

'What else do you want her to do? A bit of brain surgery on the side?'

I shrugged. 'It was just that I wondered if she might be a bit – bored?'

'Never mentioned it to me.'

It was clear I wasn't endearing myself to him; in any case there were more important things to talk about, once we'd finished eating.

'Is there any way of learning if Andy's arrived safely wherever it is?' I asked at last.

'Where's your phone?'

I gestured to the living room. He pulled himself to his feet, and plodded off: I half-expected him to close the door behind him, but he didn't. There was no way of hearing what he said without shamelessly eavesdropping, so I simply gathered up the eggy plates and shoved them into the dishwasher – let that new powder I was using prove its efficacy. Come to think of it, it had to clean yesterday's eggy plates too, complete with bacon fat. That would really be a challenge.

He was back before I could switch it on.

'They've arrived safely. Ruth's a bit knocked-up, that's all.'

'I suppose I couldn't talk to Andy?'

'Hardly. I haven't spoken to *them*, Sophie, just to an intermediary, who called them earlier. A simple precaution, in case anyone happens to be interested in your phone calls.'

'Jesus.' I sat down heavily.

'What's up, kid?'

'Sorry. Don't mean to be stupid, over such a little thing. It's just that someone bugged my house and my office last spring. I—'

'Come on, now.' He patted my shoulder. 'I don't reckon it's the thought of being bugged that's doing this to you. It's all yesterday's goings-on. Though it's not nice being bugged, of course. Not that you're bugged now. Checked it over while you were still sending your pigs to market.'

'I don't snore!' I sat upright. 'And how did you check, anyway?'

'Let's just say I didn't have to crawl round on my hands

and knees. Science and technology, Sophie. Now, how d'you propose to spend the rest of the day?'

'Marking,' I said, horribly promptly.

It suited him to spend the day lying low; it would, he observed, be a real bummer for anyone hoping for some action. Not that we could see any cars or vans loitering with or without intent. And the only telephone calls were from my friends. We both found ourselves drawn to live football on TV in the afternoon, watching – in my case with despair – West Bromwich Albion courting defeat with some determination. He enjoyed the roast lamb I cooked for supper. I marked some more. He watched TV some more.

The following morning I was required to wave him a very public goodbye as, bewigged again and looking every inch the rock star, he got into a taxi, the exhaust emissions of which would have acted as highly effective a smoke-screen had he wanted one. He headed off to New Street Station – in theory, at least – and I went off to work, wondering if I would miss his stolidly comforting presence. I should have taught like a dream, secure in the knowledge that West Midlands Police were conducting post mortems, initiating forensic science examinations of the contents of Andy's flask, seeking what I knew in my heart of hearts was a murderer. Instead I found myself staring bleakly from the windows, as if being on the fifteenth floor cut me off from more areas of life than I'd ever imagined.

Chapter Nine

Gurjit, having knocked deferentially at the staff room door, found me just as I was piling my sandwiches and apple on top of a heap of papers for a lunch-time meeting. Monday morning with a vengeance! My agenda had gone astray, and I couldn't for the life of me recall having ever seen the minutes of the last meeting; someone had boiled the staff room kettle dry, and the nearest machine was on the eighth floor – at the far end of the earth when you're five minutes late for a meeting on the fifteenth. In any case the chances were someone would have jammed it up with superglued metal discs. I'd have to manage without a drink.

'Gurjit!' I managed to find a smile.

'My parents,' she began, 'have been kind enough to give their consent.'

I must have looked blank.

'The airport work experience,' she explained. 'They've given permission for me to take up the offer. Since I seem to be on top of my assignments at the moment, it would seem sensible to start this week if possible.'

I nodded. 'I'll phone Mark Winfield to set it up as soon as I can. Later this afternoon, probably. Could you pop back about five?'

'My class finishes at four,' she said. 'My parents expect me straight back.'

At least now that she had a car her father wasn't sitting outside in his Mercedes, waiting for her to emerge from the building the moment classes finished.

‘I’ll phone you at home then – tell me your number.’ I grabbed a pencil.

‘We’re ex-directory.’ She looked distraught.

‘Well, you’ll have to tell me then.’

‘I could phone you.’

‘I’m ex-directory too,’ I snapped. ‘Do you want this work experience or not?’

Her eyes filled. What was this job turning me into?

We agreed that she would come to see me the following morning before classes began.

I could hardly explain the reason for my delay to Richard, who was chairing the meeting. He looked pointedly at his watch as I arrived, particularly as my apple chose that moment to leap from my hand and rebound from one end of the room to the other.

I managed to get hold of Mark Winfield at about five-thirty.

‘You remember that drink we’d organised? Well—’

‘You will be able to come?’

‘Yes! Of course. It’s just that I’ve got a student for you, and I wondered – well, she ought to see the place and all it involves before she commits herself.’

‘Hm. I suppose it makes sense. OK. Look here—’ He broke off; I could hear another voice in the background. ‘Sorry, Sophie – there’s a bit of a crisis. See you tomorrow, eh?’

When I finally tried to squeeze out of the car park, the traffic was solid to Five Ways, so I decided to turn towards Handsworth and back via City Road, a route circuitous and not entirely lovely, but preferable to sitting pumping carbon dioxide and goodness knows what else into the atmosphere. But traffic was slow there, too. A cheery voice on Classic FM told me there’d been a diesel spillage on the A4123 in Warley, so presumably all this chaos was the tailback from that. Miles and miles of hot, frustrated cars and drivers, all watching their windscreen wipers slapping backwards and forwards against the mean, vicious drizzle. And me in the middle of them.

At least I could take advantage of my position and push further still from home to Smethwick High Street. Most of the shops were still open, which made parking a bit of a pig. I hoped it was worth it for a little vegetable shopping. Yes: lovely fresh aubergines jostled coriander and methi. I bought three bunches of both to pick over, chop and freeze. Then a shameless dive into a Indian sweet shop for a bag of halva, jalabi, and gulab jamans.

Back along Bearwood Road the traffic thickened again, but the police had taken control of the lights, so at least those of us on the Outer Circle could cross the traffic, solid on the A456. I took my usual dodge route, picking my way round the Beech Lanes Estate. As I slowed at the last give-way sign, it occurred to me that I hadn't chafed against the delays because I didn't especially want to go home.

But it was all right. The intruder light obligingly switched on as I walked up the path; the door was still deadlocked, the burglar alarm chirruped as soon as I opened the door. Post on the mat; a couple of messages on the answering machine. Home.

Dropping my goodies on the kitchen table I went back for the post. The phone calls were from Dillons, saying some CDs I'd ordered were waiting for me – and from Carl, a William Murdock colleague who persisted in paying me attentions. This time he had a reasonable excuse for phoning, as I found out when I called back: he'd been asked to help run an Environmental Studies field trip, and many of the Asian girls could only go if there was a woman present. The trip itself would normally be the province of Beth, who taught the subject; he'd agreed to go simply as an extra whipper-in. Now, however, Beth had succumbed to the breakdown many of us had long predicted, and her doctor had signed her off for three weeks, with the probability of many more to follow. So now Carl was suddenly in charge of the trip – no mean feat for a Pharmacy lecturer – and in need of a woman. It all sounded convoluted to me, and I had a strong suspicion that Carl's wife would find it hard to credit.

'Wouldn't it be simpler to cancel the trip?' I asked.

'Course work,' he said. 'Has to be assessed.'

By whom? I couldn't rid myself of the idea that Carl was being disingenuous, but on the grounds that he no longer dropped his voice tenderly every time he spoke to me, I agreed. Provisionally. A lot could happen in a week, after all.

When I got back, the coriander was already filling the kitchen with that scent I always see as spring-green. A cup of tea: then I'd deal with the post and then cook. The coriander could soak out its sand in the sink while I ate.

Except I didn't feel like eating when I'd read the mail. 'Read' is an exaggeration. All I had to do was look at a sexually explicit caricature of Andy, mutilated with gusto.

Ian had responded to my panicky phone call. He sat opposite me, sipping Tio Pepe.

'If you carry on swilling that stuff,' he said, touching the Jameson's with his index finger, 'you'll start to lose your palate. Before a meal, too.'

He was right, of course. I got up and put the bottle away, reaching for the mineral water instead. He nodded approvingly.

'I'll pass this on to the boss,' he said, touching the caricature which he'd already slipped into a transparent polythene bag. The envelope was in another.

'Thought so,' I said, pointing at the second bag. 'Posted last Thursday, before the Music Centre business. I wonder where it's been lurking till now.'

'Wherever second-class post lurks. I wonder why Chummie didn't send it first-class?'

'Poor? Or mean? Oh, Ian, why are they doing this to Andy? There isn't a nicer man on God's earth.'

He looked unconvinced.

'Come on! Ruth wouldn't have married him if he hadn't been a good guy.' Not often I serve an ace.

'I wish young Chris was back here,' he said. 'She's not a bad lass, young Diane Stephenson, but she hasn't Chris's clout with them upstairs. They tell her they can't afford something, she believes them. Chris would spend all night preparing a set of figures to prove they could – and get the other resources he wanted to boot.'

'She seems to be under a lot of pressure,' I said.

'Well, she would be. Only acting Inspector. Can't afford to put a foot wrong, can she? Though it's my experience that when you most try to avoid things, you always seem to trample on them.'

I topped up his sherry and my water. 'Like Christmas tree lights and people's toes?'

'Exactly. No more for me after this, love – I'm driving, remember. You're looking peaky. What are you doing about food?'

'I've got a load of stuff in the freezer – I did some batch cooking over Christmas.'

He stood up. 'Now, you'll lock up after me, won't you? And check under your car tomorrow? Not that it's you they're after – but you never know.'

Tuesday was an inordinately long day. I taught from nine till one, and then again from one-thirty till five-thirty. Since the rush-hour traffic was bad yet again, there seemed little point in trying to go home, especially as I'd promised to give Gurjit a lift to the airport that evening. The only bright spot was the discovery of a new Italian restaurant near the Conservatoire. Not that it *was* new, of course: just new to me. I'd resigned myself to another mass-produced pizza; instead I fell, quite by chance, upon a risotto richly flavoured with coriander and a green salad laden with ripe avocado. As a rare and extravagant treat I polished off a huge portion of lemon tart, so sharp and delectable I could have murdered for the recipe. The only other eaters were a middle-aged couple tucked in one corner; from the expansiveness of their gestures their food was as good as mine. The chef, who had doubled as waiter, talked with passion about coriander and then waved me goodbye as if I were an old friend.

So I was in a much better frame of mind – until I returned to College. Those of us in the fifteen-floor staff room sometimes manage a rota for picking up each other's post from the general office on the eighth floor; but more often we don't. As I had just consumed more calories in one meal than I normally would in a week, I decided to walk up the stairs; the eighth floor made a convenient resting place. *Convenient*! I was so out of condition that I couldn't possibly have made it to the fifteenth without stopping. There was a fistful of mail in my pigeon-hole, which I sorted before setting off again. Notices of several meetings; minutes for several more; messages from employers about work experience. Junk mail – almost any advertising matter comes under that category if the college it's sent to can't afford even the paper for exams. Two requests for references from past students looking for work. And two envelopes tightly sealed with tape, addressed in Karen's undistinguished fist.

Two?

I sat down at one of the vacant desks, using a canteen knife smelling strongly of oranges to slit the first envelope open. Then the second envelope: this scrawl related to her 'earlier note'. 'Note' was a distinct misnomer: epistle, more like. I went back to the first. Ostensibly, it was a thank-you letter for Saturday; in reality it was a paean of praise for Andy – his looks, his kindness, his compassion. Would I pass on her thanks – or better still, pass on the enclosed letter? That accounted for some of the envelope's fatness – there was another 'note' for Andy sealed – and taped – in with the first. On, then, to letter number two. This was a reprise of number one, except that she would now be too embarrassed for Andy to see the first letter, so would I destroy it and pass on this one instead? She'd asked the secretary to return her first letter to me, but . . .

Confused, and not altogether interested in her protestations of undying love for my cousin, I gathered the whole pile together and resumed my journey upwards. And damn me if there wasn't another note, on my desk, also sealed with tape, saying she needed to be alone and, in her absence, asking me to destroy all her letters. Preferably burn them. I thought the shredder might do, but it seemed to be jammed, and rather than trudge back down to the eighth I decided to leave it till morning. I shoved them into my in-tray, under the agendas and minutes, so that no one else would read them and see what a cake she was making of herself.

There was just time to finish marking a pile of assignments well overdue for return. But, at this point Gurjit arrived. I suppose her promptness – she was half an hour early – augured well for her work experience, but at the moment it merely meant a kicking of heels – hers while I ploughed through assignments, or ours while we waited for Mark, if we arrived early at the airport. In view of her obvious anxiety, compromise seemed in order, so she sat through one assignment and one repair of make-up and half an hour later we were in the airport car park, watching the little numbers hopping round on my dashboard clock.

It had turned into an unattractive night. A thin drizzle seemed to be freezing as it fell, and the wind took the absence of major obstacles as an invitation to gust so strongly that the car, usually imperturbable, started bucking sideways. The drive back through the tangle of Spaghetti Junction could well be an exciting one. Meanwhile, I had an evening of work to get through, including a foray on to a cold, wet runway – not a pleasant social evening, starting in the pub and maybe not getting much further.

Despite the wait in the car, we still presented ourselves about five minutes early. Mark greeted us affably, then allowed himself an anxious glance at his desk. 'Look – I have to complete this for tomorrow. Would you mind terribly – there's some magazines over there—'

So there were. Nice glossy ones, all about airports. Gurjit devoured the nearest: yes, she'd do well here, or anywhere else for that matter. I thought of the pile of assignments and contemplated with apprehension the prospect of getting up at six to finish marking them. I also looked at Mark, covertly. He seemed to be what might be considered an eligible young male, with, now I came to notice them, the most beautiful eyelashes. Though I didn't see myself skipping off into domesticity via a romantic sunset, there was something in what Andy had said. Companionship. Someone to cook for – or, better still, with. Someone to go to concerts and theatres with. Someone – yes – someone to go to bed with. And then I blushed. All those prepositions at the end of sentences! And me the arch-pedant of William Murdock. In any case, all this speculation was a bit on the previous side. All we'd done was chat about cricket.

Mark sighed and looked up. 'I suppose you teachers find these things easy.'

'Reports? Not intellectually challenging. But not easy.'

We exchanged a smile. Hmm. Back to professionalism, Sophie.

'Only two more minutes,' he said.

I dug in my bag for the references he'd need for Gurjit: one from me, one from her personal tutor, both testifying to her honesty and reliability. I had a letter from Richard as well, just in case. I would miss Richard quite badly, now I came to think of it. He'd been at William Murdock when I started; though we'd had the odd skirmish, largely because he considered important rules which I merely saw as a challenge, our relationship had been friendly. What would his replacement be like?

'There!' Mark said, replacing the top of his pen with a satisfied click. 'Right, we'll go and have a quick half – things won't hot up till about ten.'

'Half?' Gurjit asked.

'Down at The Flying Saucer,' he said.

'Pardon?'

'A drink at the pub. It's all right – you can have mineral water,' I said.

'I have never been in a pub,' she said, wide-eyed with panic. 'My parents—'

I believed her. Most of her contemporaries weren't so inclined to filial obedience, of course; we were used to students of all races and religions discovering the pleasures of drink in the library study carrels. All too soon the pleasures were followed by the ignominy of being sick into a waste basket and being expelled as a consequence: even the most disciplined teetotal families had to receive repentant and hung-over students back to their bosoms. Sikh, Christian, Muslim, Hindu, Jew – we'd seen the lot. But it was a long time since I'd come across a student who hadn't even been to a pub.

I caught Mark's eye.

'I can offer you tea or coffee, er, Gurjit?'

'I don't take stimulants, thank you. My religion—' She bit her lip, humiliated.

I tried to rescue her. 'Mark, I was wondering if you could show Gurjit where she'd be working, tell her roughly what she'll be expected to do. Then we could see all the action later.' I passed over the references, which he put in an envelope file.

Although I'd seen no one else around, he locked his door carefully as we left, and took care not to let us see the code he tapped to gain us admission to the outer office. And then he laughed. 'I'll have to get you to memorise that, Gurjit. You mustn't even leave the room to go to – er – the cloakroom without locking up and unlocking it again. Learn it by heart. Don't write it down anywhere. Treat it like your bank's PIN number. And don't feel tempted to tell anyone.'

'What if I forget? And there's no one to ask, like tonight?'

'OK, Sophie – you'd better know too. 1.1.44. My mother's birthday. I take it Gurjit could phone you up in a crisis?'

I bit back a tart comment about occasionally having a home-life. 'I'd rather you didn't forget, Gurjit, if it's all the same to you.'

Her work station was screened from the others; already there was a suspiciously thick pile in the in-tray. He sat down and we watched: one over either shoulder.

'Now,' he said, switching on the computer, 'this is what happens.' He tapped in another set of figures as he spoke: a little row of asterisks appeared obediently on the screen.

'Don't I need to know the password too?' she asked.

He shook his head. 'Security, I'm afraid. Someone will always start up the system for you. We can't expect Sophie to remember another set of numbers.'

Watching over his shoulder, I thought it more tactful not to tell him that that particular set would take no remembering – the series of numbers he'd tapped in was Andy's birthday.

'The system's very efficient. When a plane logs in with the

control tower we know its code. As soon as that's entered, its payload comes up on the screen – if anyone's using it – and is printed out there.'

As if on cue, a printer – a nice new laser – hummed quietly and disgorged a print-out. I went into immediate covet-mode: the minimal peace of our staff room was daily assaulted by a dot-matrix printer chugging out thirteen people's hand-outs. Since photocopy cards were at a premium at this stage of the financial year there was a great temptation to run off sets of notes, so life was dominated by the appalling clatter.

'What the duty clerk then has to do is check the print-out, log it manually, then send out an invoice to the appropriate firms. There you are – this one would go to Parcel Force. And that one. It's not very exciting work, but it's extremely responsible. If the invoices go out late, we lose money; if they go to the wrong people, we lose good will.'

'Of course. Oh, look – that firm belongs to a friend of my father's!'

'Better make sure they get the right invoice, then,' Mark said. 'Ah! It sounds as if the party's starting. Back to my office, please.'

We were rigged out in yellow day-glo waistcoats and ear-protectors; our bags were locked in Mark's safe. I set the security alarm off as we walked through into the passenger area – I'd left my keys in my pocket. I parked them ignominiously on the security counter and tried again – OK, this time. Gurjit watched with what looked suspiciously like a gleam of amusement in her eye, ostentatiously shed her bangles, passed them to Mark, and sailed through silently. His smile as he returned them to her, slipping them over her hand, had an interesting quality.

Although it had stopped raining we stayed under cover while a couple of planes landed, putting on the ear-protectors without being told. I still knew next to nothing about planes, and was amazed to hear Gurjit make some factual observation about the age of the one taxi-ing away from us. So was Mark, to judge from his expression.

'My father was in the Indian Air Force,' she said. 'He has a passion for aeroplanes. But those Viscounts must be forty years old.'

'Due for honourable retirement in some aircraft museum?' I asked.

'They're safe enough,' Mark said. 'There probably isn't much that hasn't been replaced since they started flying. In fact, you might wonder if they're really the same plane.'

Gurjit looked at him. 'But surely, Mr Winfield, all human cells are renewed on a regular basis. Does that mean that Sophie, for instance, isn't the same person as she was forty years ago?'

Forty? I opened my mouth to protest, and then realised all I would be doing was interrupting someone else's conversation.

Mark looked at her seriously. 'In terms of human cells, no. Except they all configure to make one person, guided by that individual's DNA. And humans have another characteristic that inanimate objects lack. Any ideas?'

'Personality? Memory?'

'Exactly – *hell*!' he shouted.

Simultaneously we donned ear-protectors again. Another big plane – red, with the Parcel Force logo – landed and taxi-ed in. We waited until Mark removed his protectors before doing the same.

'There – there's a plane over there just about to be unloaded. It's full of what we call igloos – see?'

I didn't see much resemblance myself, but I nodded.

'Those containers?' asked Gurjit. 'So the planes aren't full of loose cargo?'

'Loose-loaded, we call it. Some are – see that one over there, with the conveyor belt? But that system's too labour-intensive to be popular – too expensive.'

'And rather too vulnerable,' Gurjit said.

'Vulnerable?' Mark repeated.

'To theft, of course. Unless you have strict security?'

I hugged myself. Gurjit had been an inspired choice for this placement. Her face was more animated than I'd ever seen it; her voice warm with enthusiasm. And it looked as if she and Mark would get on well together. Perhaps too well for my liking.

'It is pretty strict, but you're right. Some firms seem to ask to have stuff stolen. Look at that lot over there.'

We looked at a heap of packages in transit towards what looked like a warehouse. They were all brightly taped with the firm's name.

'So if you want to steal computer equipment you know which to go for,' Gurjit said. 'Have you remonstrated with the firm?'

Mark caught my eye briefly. 'We have.'

'But they remain unconvinced?'

'Clearly!' I said.

A sudden spatter of rain made us turn with one accord for the warehouse, which turned out to be a huge postal sorting office, noisy from the metal cages holding the parcels and from the shouted conversations of the men and women working there. From there we went to an area full of large lorries playing dodgems. To get back through a hefty gate to the apron we had to be searched – a body search for Mark, despite the fact that his must be a well-known face, or perhaps because of it. They merely ran a sort of electronic baton over us women.

'Planes take off from here for all sorts of sensitive places,' Mark said.

'So, in addition to stopping people stealing from the planes, you want to stop them putting anything extra on.'

Gurjit won another smile from Mark. 'Exactly.'

Back in his office, with packets of fruit juice he'd bought from the canteen, we sat down, suddenly constrained. I was silent because all I wanted was my bed: but Mark and Gurjit sat staring at each other, he young and personable with an intriguing limp, she suddenly looking as if the black she habitually wore was a fashion decision to enhance a glowing olive skin. Except I'd never seen her skin glow before. Oh, dear . . .

'When can you start?'

'When can I start?'

They spoke simultaneously. They replied simultaneously. 'Tomorrow?'

'Good.' I said, putting down my fruit juice and peeling off the waistcoat. 'That's settled then.'

Chapter Ten

I seemed to have taught for an eternity, though my watch insisted it was only ten-thirty. Break! I got back to the office to find Ian Dale sitting at my desk, drinking a cup of tea and inspecting a pile of photographs. Shahida was at her desk, which was next to mine, actually sitting down – a most unusual posture for her, since she was usually on her feet running wherever it was she was heading. They looked up and beamed when they saw me. I gestured to Ian to stay where he was, made a mug of tea for myself and joined them, admiring the latest snaps of what was my sort-of-god-daughter. Since Shahida and her husband were Muslim, and I was a distinctly lapsed Baptist, the spiritual side of the baby's development wasn't going to figure high on my agenda, but I was keen on most other activities, especially bath-time and feeding ducks.

'There you are again, Sophie – I've never seen so many pictures of you,' Ian said.

'No, they're photos of the baby with me in them,' I said. 'I'm just the supporting cast. Hey, isn't that the bear I gave her?'

'One of them,' Shahida said.

'Like that, is she? Doting?'

'I don't dote!'

'Not much she doesn't! This is one of two identical bears, Ian, so that when one gets sicked on it can go in the wash, but Maria doesn't miss him because she can cuddle his twin brother.' Maria is a Muslim name, too – the stress goes on the first syllable.

Ian gave one of his rare smiles of approval. 'Neat, that. I remember my favourite teddy had to be thrown away. Never found another like him. Still,' he sighed heavily, 'I suppose that's life.'

Did I dare? Did I dare buy Ian a teddy bear for his birthday next month? Chris would say I couldn't possibly, that the whole idea was absurd and outrageous – but then I probably wouldn't consult him.

We nattered through the rest of the photos, my colleagues and students washing in and around us as if we were a sand-castle defying the tide. At last Shahida gathered the photos together, and set off to her next class.

Ian raised an eyebrow. 'Anywhere we can talk?'

I snorted. 'You know as well as I do there isn't! We'd better try and find a classroom – it's the best I can do unless you can requisition somewhere better.'

'Only want to give you some news, Sophie. No need for you to be so touchy.'

'Sorry. Had a late night last night,' I explained as we walked along the corridor, and told him about the airport visit. I didn't tell him that I hadn't got a sentence out of Gurjit since that didn't begin, 'Do you think Mark would . . .?' Neither did I tell him that Mark had been on the phone to me at well before nine to thank me for arranging everything so well and asking if I had Gurjit's home number so he could 'arrange a few details' with her. Since I couldn't oblige, he'd entreated me to dig her out of class as soon as she got in to ask her to phone him. Her class had proved to be on the third floor. I was so knackered I might have permitted myself to use the lifts today – except that hand-written notices were stuck on three of them announcing that they were out of order. You can imagine the crush to get into the fourth.

'No wonder you're looking peaky,' he said. 'After all the business at the weekend – ah! Is that room empty?'

Until we went in, it did indeed appear to be. Only the steady, rhythmic rocking of a bank of filing cabinets which concealed the corner hidden from the corridor suggested otherwise. Groans of what sounded like pleasure reinforced the suspicion.

'Shouldn't you do something? Report them, or something?' Ian demanded as I locked the door behind us.

'Let me see . . . We'd have to go and identify whoever it is, cough to announce our presence, witness their embarrassment – not to mention ours – wait while they got dressed, report them formally, go to a disciplinary hearing as witnesses . . .'

'OK, OK. All the same—'

'All right.' I fished a Post-It out of the depths of my bag and wrote: *Please do not use this room for this purpose again or there could be serious consequences.* Then I unlocked the door again – just, by the sound of it, at the crucial moment – stuck the note where it could not escape notice, and locked up once more. 'There. Nicely ambiguous, don't you think?'

'Humph,' said Ian, peering through another door; this room was occupied by a History teacher and a pile of marking.

At last we found the Geography room empty. Ian prowled round, apparently looking for something: since we'd spent five minutes looking for a room and I was due to teach in a further five, this time on the fourth floor, I found the delay irritating, but it never did to hurry Ian – not if you wanted the fully-rounded version of whatever he was prepared to impart.

'Brent Knoll,' he said at last, prodding a relief map. 'Contour maps of Brent Knoll – that's what we did in Geography. Some rubbish at the end of a glacier. And now it's a service station with a fancy name. Sedgemoor. Why not Brent Knoll? In memory of all of us who did Geography all those years ago. It's probably not even called Geography any more. Environmental Studies, or something.'

I waited.

'Well, they found something in that young man's body. Helleborin, that's what they think it is. Affects the eyes. And other things. Heard of it?'

I shook my head. 'In what way affects the eyes?'

He flicked open his pad. 'Photophobia and visual disturbances. Also causes vertigo and tinnitus.'

'Just the thing you want to take if you're Andy and

performing at a pop concert.' Then I started to feel sick. 'Were there any traces in Andy's flask, by any chance?'

'Still testing at the forensic science lab. But they'll be shifting on that, now we have the pathologist's report. If it was Chris in charge, we wouldn't still be waiting.'

I made an effort to concentrate. 'You did say Stephenson's in a difficult position.'

'Not in the pub, she isn't. One of those women who has to be tougher than the toughest man. The amount of whisky she sinks! Rough stuff, too. She's prepared to drink any bloke under the table. And her language! I thought you were bad enough, but she'd out-cuss you any day.'

That was the ultimate condemnation. I glanced at my watch. 'Look, I've got a class. Anything more you can tell me while we walk down the stairs? Like, where you found Andy's flask? I didn't get a chance to ask on Saturday.'

'Behind that drum kit. Absolute tip back there. You'd never have known – ' he paused, while I locked up – 'that those fellows had only been there a few hours. All sorts of muck. Disgusting. Half-eaten sarnies, cups half-full of cold coffee . . . Worse than your staff room, and that's saying something.'

'It is indeed. So what's going to happen now? How did he get hold of helleborin, whatever it is? Is it some sort of magic mushroom?'

He looked at his note book again. 'Plant extract.'

'Hallucinogenic, as well as all those other things?'

He shook his head. 'No idea. Are you thinking what I'm thinking?'

I wouldn't rush him. I *mustn't* rush him. 'What are you thinking?'

'That this bloke took a bit of something, overdid it, and Bob's your uncle. Right?'

'It was a no-drugs tour.'

'Well, perhaps he took something that no one'd know about.'

I shook my head. 'Look – some of them smoke pot, and one or two snort coke, especially the youngsters. But they get the push immediately if Jonty finds out. And no one in his right mind would take anything if he was going to be stuck up that gantry. You wouldn't expect a steeple-jack to have a quick fix, would you?'

'Ah, but these musicians—'

'Musicians, my foot. Electrical engineers. Computer experts. Family men, most of them – well, you saw at the party. That guy – did he have a wife and kids?'

'A partner. Male.' Disapproval oozed from Ian's every pore.

I wouldn't react.

'Who *says* Pete never took anything except marijuana.'

'Did they find anything else – on him? At his place?'

'You sound more like Chris every day!'

We reached the room where I was scheduled to teach. Outside my class was seething round, moaning loudly. When I peered at the door I could see why.

ROOM OCCUPIED.
GO TO ROOM 1504.

I don't like to think what expletive passed my lips.

'Problem?' asked Ian.

'None at all. Except that only one lift is working and that Room 1504 is back on the fifteenth floor. Would you call that a problem?'

At lunch-time I wanted simply to put my head down and go to sleep, but there was a Board of Study meeting I had to attend. Since the Board's intention was to make me a scapegoat for the ongoing lack of success of the work experience programme, I drank strong black coffee beforehand and flourished sets of figures. My colleagues were normally tolerant, kindly people, fraught with the same stresses as I – but put them in a room and call them a committee and they became steely-eyed and officious. However, my impressive lists convinced them that I'd done all I could to find placements in an period when employers were besieged with requests; and that my in-college campaign to persuade students to take up the meagre supply of placements had failed because of the students' apathy, as personified by the student rep on the committee.

'Waste of time, innit,' he said. 'I goes to her, I goes to Sophie, there's no work to go to, innit? And she goes to me, she's trying. But I goes to her, I goes, she don't find the right places anyway, innit – I mean, ought to be with lawyers or accountants, innit.'

The Head of English sighed audibly – and I knew I had been reprieved. Student literacy might well appear on the agenda for the next Board meeting: I might even chime in myself, with an observation on the use of the verb 'to go' as a verb of saying.

Late for my one-fifteen class, I still found only a quarter of the usual complement there. Their serious faces and plethora of textbooks told me I had promised them a test; naturally I postponed it until I could trawl a bigger catch, and set instead a comprehension exercise that would take them for ever. While they read it through and listed words they didn't know, I leaned on the window sill, trying to stop my heart pounding as though I were in a race. Pete Hughes and helleborin. Visual disturbances. Auditory interference. No trace of any substances on him or at home . . . There *had* to be a message from Ian waiting for me back in the staff room. Had to be. And it would tell me that they'd found helleborin in Andy's flask. The suspicion that had nagged so strongly on Saturday – the one Griff shared – must be proved a fact: one I didn't want, now it came to it, to face. There would be poison in Andy's flask because it was Andy for whom it was meant.

At break, over the phone, Ian's voice, normally prosaic and flat, alternated between excitement at what seemed to him a new development and concern for me.

'The trouble is, love, we need to talk to Andy and he seems to have disappeared from the face of the earth. Get him to come back to Brum, just for a couple of days, will you?'

'Can't. Don't know where he is.'

'Come off it, love. This is serious.'

'It's my bloody cousin, and someone wants to kill him, and you tell me it's serious! Of *course* it's serious! But I don't know how to reach him. He's in hiding, Ian.'

'Don't tell me he didn't tell you where he was going.'

'I – what is it? Can't you see I'm on the phone? Just one second, Ian.' I covered the mouthpiece. 'I'm busy, Karen. Wait a minute, please.'

'I can't. It's so *important*?'

'Two minutes. And wait outside. This is personal.'

'Is it Andy? Sophie, tell him—'

'Outside!' I watched her almost stagger from the room. What on earth was wrong with the girl? 'Ian, I'm sorry. Look, John Griffiths – his minder – left me his card. I can get him to contact Andy, make him contact you. That's truly the best I can do.'

There was a long silence.

'You're telling the truth, aren't you? You really don't know.'

It was the first time in thirty-five years I didn't. He'd always carried my name on his dog-tag as next of kin: now he would have Ruth's.

'Give me Griff's number, will you, love?' His voice was distressingly kind. 'Thanks. Now, Val's trying out that lamb casserole recipe you gave her – how'd you like to come round this evening and see how she's got on with it?'

'Love to, Ian,' I lied. 'But I've got to do another work experience visit on the way back, and goodness knows how long it will take.'

In fact I had to go and see Naheeda, the student who'd alleged misconduct against her temporary employer. It was an assignment I was not looking forward to, but anything was better than Ian being tactful. I picked my way through the late afternoon traffic to Hockley, nosing through increasingly mean streets to the two-up two-down house. I rang gently, knocked gently; then did both less gently. At last an old man emerged from the house next door, wearing a round fleecy cap, black waistcoat and white pyjama-like shirt and trousers of a thin cotton fabric. My heart bled for him: he must have been in danger of hypothermia.

‘I wanted to see Naheeda,’ I said, turning in to the wind to face him, pulling strands of hair from my eyes and mouth.

‘Naheeda gone,’ he said, making a palms-down scissors movement with his hands. ‘Gone Pakistan.’

‘Pakistan! But she goes to college!’

‘Naheeda gone Pakistan. Marry.’

‘But she’s only seventeen!’

‘Marry in Pakistan.’ He infused a frightening note of satisfaction into his voice. ‘Gone.’ A final scissors movement with his hands, and he was gone too, his sandals flapping on bare feet. I found myself hoping he’d get chilblains.

Back on the road again, I missed my way and found myself heading into the city rather than round it. Cursing my stupidity, I tried to work out which possible route might have the fewest jams, and decided to surface on Great Charles Street, so I could leave the city on Broad Street. Then I could choose – if the Five Ways Island was solid I could risk the underpass and the Hagley Road. There would be plenty of time to decide. The traffic had slowed to breathing pace – a combination of cars turning right and others illegally parked. It was fortunate that it was then I decided to test the Renault’s front bumper.

I saw Andy, you see. Nipping across the pedestrian crossing by the Music Centre.

I apologised profusely to the Volvo driver in front, who’d inspected every last centimetre for possible damage – though even my little bumper was unscathed, I’d touched so lightly – and when I at last found somewhere to park, Andy was nowhere to be seen. Of course. I told myself, as I fastened myself back into the Renault, that my eyes must have deceived me, that in the dazzle of the lights and the gentle sleet I couldn’t have recognised anyone. That from the back Phiz looked like Andy – and so, with a wig, did Griff. So, probably did hundreds of men. That Andy was somewhere safe in the north. That no one with any sense would return from a safe house to a place where someone was trying to kill him.

But I knew those shoulders, the set of that head, that walk, better than I knew my own.

Chapter Eleven

Trying to prise information out of Griff was predictably tough. He insisted that Andy – he referred to him only as 'our friend' – would be where he was supposed to be. When I floated as the merest possibility a journey south, he tried very hard not to tell me to be a fool; while he censored his words, he couldn't quite control his voice. Since I could scarcely spell out exactly whom I had seen and where, lest there be any unwanted listeners, I tried hard not to blame him. At the end I wrung from him a grudging promise to talk to 'another friend' – his contact, presumably – and call me back.

It naturally became one of those evenings when all your friends phone expecting a long natter. I'd never quite got round to having BT signal another caller, and so my enjoyment was spoilt by the constant suspicion that someone with vital information was being denied access to me.

So I heard all about the problems Aberlene was having with her new bloke, who seemed to resent her being the leader of the Midshires Symphony Orchestra while he was only a back-desk second violin. *All* about them. I managed after half an hour to suggest we should meet to discuss it – a girls' evening at a nice restaurant. There was a little, hurt pause.

Then I remembered that itinerant musicians saw more restaurants than the rest of us.

'Or how about a meal here?' I suggested.

We found a date and wrote solemnly in our diaries.

Carl next: why he hadn't contacted me at work goodness

knows. His wife had suspected that we were lovers years before we actually were, and presumably still regarded me with suspicion, though I'd given her no grounds for nearly two years now. So why should he take the risk of phoning me? Was it simply to enrage a not-very-nice woman? All he wanted to talk about was our 'expedition' – his word, not mine – up the River Severn. He read out the instruction leaflet he'd prepared, asked me what I thought of his check-list of essential items, speculated on the likely state of the weather, and generally irritated the socks off me.

My hand was poised to phone Griff when another call came through, this time from college. *College*? One of my colleagues, an historian, had found this student in tears outside the staffroom . . .

It had to be Karen. Surely she hadn't been waiting there all that time . . . *No, don't be silly, Sophie.*

'She says she has to talk to you. She says – I'll put her on, shall I?'

'OK, Mags – but don't tell her my number!'

'Sophie? Sophie? I've got to talk to you, I really have. Sophie, it's about Andy . . . Have you sent him my letters?'

'No. You asked me to destroy them.' I didn't mention that I hadn't yet got round to it.

'But Sophie – I need – he must – '

She must be deadly serious: she'd dropped that inter-rogation.

'Must what, Karen?' Keep the voice calm – that's what they taught on counselling courses.

'*Talk* to him! Sophie, I *must*.'

'That's not possible at the moment, love. He's not in Birmingham.'

'He is, he is! I *saw* him!'

Where? *Where*? No – mustn't scream down the phone at a student. I said nothing.

'I *saw* him,' she insisted.

'Are you sure? When did you think you saw him?'

'This afternoon. I *saw* him. Why won't you let me speak to him?'

'Because – ' I might as well tell her the simple truth – 'he's on holiday with Ruth and I don't have a clue where.'

'You're lying! You don't want him to know how much I love him! You're *jealous*!'

She cut the line abruptly. The phone rang again almost immediately.

Mags again. 'Wow! Something seems to have upset her, Sophie. What d'you want me to do? Apart from wring her neck, that is?'

'Would you be an absolute angel and get out her personal file? Oh, hell, you can't, can you?' One of the recent funding changes meant that all the students' files now had to be kept centrally: I wasn't quite sure how, or why, except that the change was accompanied by an inordinate amount of form-filling. Everything we did for our students was now documented, allegedly so we could claim money for it, but somewhere along the way the notion of instant access had been lost. And it is a truth inadequately acknowledged, that every single tutee in possession of a problem must be in want of comfort outside college hours. 'I just wanted her phone number, to let her mother know she's in a state.'

'Are you sure she isn't eighteen?'

'Doesn't behave like it!'

'Maybe not, but you can only contact parents if they're sixteen or seventeen. Rules is rules.'

'Yes, Mags. But it's all a bit academic, isn't it, if we can't find her telephone number anyway?'

What was the girl's surname? Harris? There were an awful lot of Harrises in the phone book, and since I'd no more than the vaguest idea of her address – somewhere in Acocks Green, wasn't it? – that was that. The best I could do was go chasing tomorrow, first thing.

Next came ActionAid, asking me to do a door-to-door collection. Then a couple of wrong numbers. Ten o'clock – and still no news from Griff.

At five past I was startled out of the ITN News by a strident ring at my front door. A peep through the spy-hole showed Inspector Stephenson, with Ian two paces behind.

She said, without preamble, as soon as she set foot in the hall, 'I have to talk to your cousin. Sergeant Dale tells me you're not co-operating.'

'Hang on a sec,' I said, literally scratching my head.

'Surely you people must know where he's staying. You had the name and address of everyone connected with the – the incident, didn't you? You can't have let us all go swanning off our separate ways without knowing where to find us if things developed.' I shut the door, and gestured less than politely to the living room.

Ian stood aside to let her pass. Catching a gust of whisky, I asked brightly, 'Coffee, everyone?'

'Too late for me, love. Ta all the same.'

'Black, please.'

Too late for me, too. But I find it's never too late for a chocolate biscuit.

By the time I'd made coffee – instant, it has to be admitted – I had given her enough time to work out a response to my question.

You're sure,' she said, taking the mug carefully, 'that you've had no contact with your cousin?'

'Only via John Griffiths. As I'm sure he told you, Griff thought the fewer people who knew Andy's whereabouts the better. And that included me. What's the problem?'

'Peter Hughes fell to his death after consuming enough helleborin to cause significant visual and auditory disturbance. Not enough to kill him: it was the fall that did that. We have found no trace of helleborin anywhere other than in your cousin's flask. We need to establish when and why the helleborin entered the flask. Especially why.'

'So that it would have the same effect on Andy, surely!'

'I'm not sure I understand you, Ms Rivers.'

'Sophie, please. So that he would experience the same symptoms as Pete Hughes. Except – hang on – Andy never goes anywhere near a gantry, does he? He'd have fallen over on stage. It would have looked as if he was – '

'I'm not convinced,' she cut in. 'I suspect Mr Rivers may have used illegal substances to energise himself for the concert: herbal ones, rather than the more obvious substances he publicly denounces.'

'Inspector Stephenson,' I said, with a creditable attempt at patience, 'do you not recall our telling you about all the other little incidents? The obituary, the vandalism, and so on? You even offered to increase security on the night of the concert. Can't we return to the theory you appeared to espouse then – that someone is trying to kill – or at very least damage – a man whose sole aim in life now is to improve the lot of countless Africans?'

The rhetoric wasn't entirely spurious. I wanted to return her to her mood of Saturday afternoon.

'Remember,' I urged, 'that call from the Press Association. Someone had obviously tipped them the wink that Andy was dead.'

Ian got up and thoughtfully nipped a dying leaf from my winter cherry plant.

'Whatever the reason, I need to speak to him and I need to speak to him now,' Stephenson said.

'I suggest you try your contact number for him, then.'

At this point the phone rang; I snatched it up.

'Sophie? Griff.'

What a moment to choose!

'Any news of our friend?' I asked.

'Plenty. All bad. Only sodding well slipped his leash, hasn't he?'

'Leash!'

'Flit the coop. Had a phone call, kissed Miss Jean Roadie goodbye, and said he'd got to see a man about a dog – be back for tea on Saturday. This being Wednesday, he has enough time to see a hell of a lot of dogs.'

'What does Ruth say?'

'Nothing. Voice still out of use. She writes nothing, either. So where does that leave us, eh, Sophie?'

'Helping,' I said grimly, trying desperately not to cry, 'the police with their enquiries.'

Chapter Twelve

I would try to contact Karen first thing the following morning, Thursday. That meant an A-Level English class from nine to twelve-fifteen – one of the high points of my week since the students, mostly women, were mature and actually wanted to learn. I didn't like being even a few minutes late for them, since several had organised immensely complicated child-care back-up to ensure they were on time. What I had to do, then, was get in bright and early, find where Karen was supposed to be for her first class, and leave a message with whoever was teaching her saying that I'd like to see her at break. That meant, of course, getting access to her file. Staff room, fifteenth floor; classroom, tenth floor; office where the files were kept, eighth floor. No problem.

Provided there were lifts.

At least getting in at the crack of dawn meant I got through the traffic easily and found an accessible parking slot: a distinct plus. But an ominous minus: I was parked alongside not one, but two, lift company cars. The engineers took pity on me and let me go up with them in the last functioning lift as far as the tenth; and then that too stopped.

Eight o'clock. I could sail through my preparation and still have plenty of time to sort out Karen. There was no point in trying to get access to her file until eight-forty at the very earliest. Administrators were the unsung heroes of William Murdoch, now the Further Education Funding Council Paper Chase was on, but they worked in general normal office hours, not the *ad hoc* ones visited on the teaching staff.

Nor was there any point in trying to raise Griff for the latest news on Andy: he'd made it clear that he would contact me as soon as he heard anything. I could scarcely ring Ian, in case it flushed out Stephenson. All I could tell myself as consolation was that if Andy wanted me, he knew where to find me. He'd even talked his way through college security on one famous occasion, when he had little more than an hour between flights and wanted to give me a fresh pineapple he'd acquired; I never did tell him it shot from being hard as the devil's head to soggy and rotting with no intervening state of just-rightness. I'd have given a lot to have him appear right now bearing a rotten pear. ??? apple. A very great deal.

If I'd been hoping for some sort of communication from Karen, to save me the pleasures of all those stairs, I was disappointed. There was the usual mess on my desk one of these days I would have to set aside an afternoon to uncover the wood that lurked under all that paper.

Right: preparation. *Dubliners.* Entrapment.

The telephone. Andy?

No. Nor Griff, nor Ian. A woman's voice I vaguely recognised but found hard to place.

'It's Julyarris.'

'I'm sorry?'

'It's Julyarris! Karenarris's mum.'

'I'm sorry?' I prompted her. Then it dawned. Mrs Harris. Karen's mother.

'I should think you are! If it hadn't been for you putting ideas into her head, none of this would have happened.'

Despite myself, my pulse speeded and I felt sick. What had I said? What had I done? Nothing! All I'd ever done for Karen was introduce her to Andy and then have them photographed together – in the company of her mother, moreover. Not guilty.

I put my voice into cool, professional mode. 'Let's start again, Mrs Harris. Firstly, what has happened?'

'She never came home last night. Been mooning around ever since Saturday, she has.'

'Mooning around?'

'You know – all weepy and dreamy. And then she phoned and said she was going to find him.'

'*Him*?'

'That cousin of yours. I mean, he's a nice enough lad—'

'She phoned you? When?'

'Last night. She was crying, couldn't stop crying – and she said she'd phoned you and you'd been ever so unkind.'

I hoped she didn't hear my indignant sigh. *Unkind*? All I'd done was tell her the simple truth.

'I hope you're pleased with yourself! A young girl looking to you for help and you turn your back on her.'

'What sort of help did she want?'

But the woman was sobbing.

Hell. A teenage girl not returning home: everyone's nightmare scenario. My head was already racing with strategies to find Karen. For one thing, I couldn't imagine the press letting slip an opportunity to bash an uncaring teacher. Poor Richard. All he wanted was a quiet life for a couple of months. And I'd forgotten I ought to talk to him about Naheeda . . .

'Mrs Harris? Mrs Harris, have you told the police yet? Because—'

'Police! They're a lot of use!'

'I think they just might be in a situation like this. Just stay where you are – I'll get a friend of mine in the force to phone you at once.'

Ian, solid to the point of being impregnable – he'd be ideal. I had both his home and his work number. Choosing the latter I tapped so fast I mis-dialled and had to start again.

When at last I got through I explained as tersely as I could what Mrs Harris had said. 'I know you're nothing to do with missing persons,' I added, 'and normally I wouldn't dream of bothering you, but—'

'I know. You'd talk it through with Chris if he was here, wouldn't you?'

I let that pass. 'It's just this obsession Karen's got all of a sudden for Andy – I'm really concerned. Concerned for her safety, of course.'

'And ever so slightly watching your back in case her family starts making trouble for you at college, eh, Sophie? Come on – I wasn't born yesterday.'

Was it just a greyish conscience? 'Guilty. But most of all I want that kid found,' I said truthfully. 'Involvement with a man who's been receiving death threats sounds dangerous to me. Involvement at *any* level.'

'Hmm. Now, let me get this straight so I can tell Her Nibs. What's the connection between you and Andy and this kid?'

'She was with me when I ran into Andy in town the other day. She went doo-lally – you know what kids are. Anyway, she wanted to see his concert and I managed to wangle her a job backstage.'

'Doing what?'

'She was a washer-up. But she spent a lot of time in the kitchen, flirting with the caterers and with Andy's chef.' I stopped abruptly: I didn't want to give anyone the idea I was terribly close to having myself. 'She left a couple of notes for me to pass to him – and another one asking me to burn them all. And last night she phoned in tears, wanting me to let her talk to him.'

'Which you couldn't, not knowing where he is.'

'Ian, I may not in the past have been entirely honest on occasion, but I've never lied to you or Chris. I wish I knew where he is—'

'OK, love. Give me her phone number. You're right – this isn't really my bag, but I'll either find someone whose bag it is or pretend it's mine. How about that?'

'No one could ask for more, Ian.'

So there was no need to hare round looking for Karen. But now I had to update Richard on developments that could only hinder his downhill trundle to retirement. Having a student despatched to Pakistan, possibly as an indirect result of something that happened while she was in our care, was bad enough; losing one through a crush on the cousin of one of your less conventional members of staff was even worse. I couldn't predict how he'd react.

He took one look at my face, gestured at the more comfortable of the visitor's chairs, and poured me nectar from his percolator. Then, as I'd hoped, he fished in his deepest drawer for his treasury of chocolate biscuits. The trouble was, I was braced for a bollocking; to my embarrassment, and even more to his, his unexpected kindness made me cry. The poor man didn't know what to do. While I burrowed for tissues, I could sense him opening files, rearranging items on his desk, trying to keep an appropriate distance – when what I'd really have liked was a quasi-avuncular arm round my shoulders.

I made an effort. 'Sorry. You'll have to stop being nice to me. Did they appoint your replacement yesterday?'

He blinked at the change of subject, then looked grim. 'I suppose it'll become common knowledge soon enough. You remember there were two jobs up? Two Heads of Department, mine for A-Level and GCSE, and Don's for NVQ and GNVQ? Well, they've merged them. One man's been appointed to run the lot.'

'I suppose it's logical, the way everyone's talking about post-sixteen education,' I said cautiously.

'Of course it is. But to change the job description on the day of the interviews? I don't know what the boss was thinking of. Worrall usually plays things absolutely by the book. The Principal with principles – you know the joke. Oh, Sophie, the sooner I've gone the better.'

I wasn't the only one who needed a shoulder to cry on.

I'd just finished the A-Level class; we'd romped through the story about Mrs Moonie, who dealt with moral problems like a butcher deals with meat – with a cleaver. A couple of women had hung back to talk to me about their last piece of homework, and another wanted to discuss the assignment I'd just set, so I was quite late back to the staff room. Twenty-five minutes before the next class, then a quick dive out to a centre for the disabled, where another of our students was on a placement: but not yet.

Gurjit was waiting for me outside the staff room: her smile was perfunctory. 'I need to talk to you,' she said, 'on a matter of the most extreme urgency.'

I could not resist looking at my watch.

'It is extremely serious,' she said reproachfully.

We found a room with little difficulty, this being the lunch-break, and I suggested she sit down opposite me at the teacher's table. She pulled a student's chair from behind a table, wrinkled her nose at the graffiti she found on it, and sat down.

'Sophie, it is about my work at the airport. There is a most serious problem.'

I'd known there would be. But I didn't want to believe that Mark had committed any sexual offence. I found I was pushing my hands towards Gurjit, fingers up, palms towards her, as if to fend off the truth. No, it had to be confronted.

'Tell me.' The counselling courses instruct you how to sit: leaning forward companionably. So that was how I sat.

'I believe,' she said slowly, but not hesitantly, 'that theft is being committed against one of the organisations using the airport.'

God help me – I nearly said, 'Is that all?' Instead, I pulled myself together. 'Theft? Why do you think that, Gurjit?' I mustn't sound judgemental, disbelieving.

'Because the figures don't add up. Incomings versus out-goings.'

'What scale of theft?'

'I don't know yet. One or two items per consignment.'

'Are you sure it isn't just a mistake? That the missing items won't be sent on later?'

She gestured dismissively. 'The figures suggest – no, I think it's regular. It's fraud. I know how it's being done, but I don't know who's doing it.'

'Have you told the airport people? Mark Winfield?'

Her eyes filled with tears. 'I – I don't want—'

What didn't she want? To risk having him laugh at her? To risk discovering his guilt? But my imagination was running too fast.

'Don't want what, Gurjit?'

She swallowed audibly, and fought to control her emotion. 'Want to make a fool of myself – if I'm wrong. I – Mark—'

'You value his good opinion of you?' I asked, as gently as I could.

Bending over her shoulder bag to hide her face, she nodded. Oh, dear.

'What evidence do you have?' I asked, all business-like.

She straightened up again. 'I didn't want to print it out. Someone might have noticed, or noticed me bringing it out.'

If only my brain would work! Chris – not his area, even if he hadn't been at Bramshill. What about Dave Clarke, an inspector in the Fraud Squad? He was up to his eyes with preparations for a big insider-dealing case; and moreover his eyes always had a predatory gleam when they shone in my direction. Not really enough excuse, if Gurjit was serious – but enough for now.

'Sophie – couldn't *you* come and look?'

'Me! I don't know the first thing about accounts!'

'No, but I know enough to teach you. To explain, at least. Please! You have to come and visit me anyway, to see how I'm getting on. Please!'

I sighed. 'When are you due in next?' *Please God, don't let it be tonight.*

'Next week. But Mark said I could go in any time. I thought perhaps tomorrow—'

'No.' My voice was so emphatic, she looked up, startled. 'No. If there is anything going on, then it's important to behave as normal.' Almost as an afterthought, I added, 'So what's being stolen? Booze, cigarettes? The usual high-duty stuff?'

She shook her head. 'Medicines.'

Before I could summon up any intelligent questions, a scream came ricocheting up the stairwell. Then another. In my book theft gives way to violence: I was hurtling down the stairs before I knew it. Two floors down, there was a pool of blood. It wasn't occupied by anyone, so I supposed that whoever had left it there was walking wounded. There was a trail of bloodspots downwards; I followed it to the eighth floor. Richard's secretary, an imperturbable woman from St Kitt's who was wearing her violet contact lenses as opposed to her turquoise or green ones, was pulling on rubber gloves and looking weary. An Afro-Caribbean lad was clutching a wad of lint to his ear. A distant emergency vehicle was getting closer.

'What happened?' I asked.

'I was bloody knifed, Miss, that's what. Fucking Pakis!'

Florence flicked her eyes heavenwards. 'It may have had something to do with the fact that you bottled him last week. Now sit still and let me look at that properly. The police and ambulance are on their way, Sophie.'

'It's that bad? Shit!' I said, suddenly realising that I'd shed Gurjit *en route.*

'Thought you were going to give up swearing for Lent,' Florence said. 'You were lucky, Earl, it's a very clean cut. Not like what you did to him. Ah!'

I turned; the lift doors opened to reveal the community copper and a couple of paramedics. What really interested me was the suggestive intonation with which the constable told Florence he'd need to talk to her later, and the little flutter of her smile when she agreed. Someone's day was going to become a bit brighter. I grinned, thought briefly of my lunch; but I knew I had to contact Gurjit, and, thanking goodness that it too was on the eighth floor, headed off to the office where the students' records were kept to find where her afternoon class would be. Twelfth floor: and mine was on the thirteenth. No problem. Better to exercise the legs than the blood-pressure. But then I looked at my watch and pressed the up button, and waited. And waited.

'What's this, Sophie? I thought you always used the stairs,' said Florence, coming up behind me on her way back from the loo. She'd taken the opportunity to put on fresh lipstick, add a little mascara, and spray herself liberally with Tendre Poison.

'Just thought I'd treat myself,' I said.

'Well, you'll have to save it for another day.'

'But the engineers were in earlier! And they'd got them working by break!'

'And the first one gave up as soon as they left the car park. Together with the one that hadn't been broken in the first place.'

I was late for my class and still hungry. I took a mug of tea in with me but rather drew the line at eating bread, cheese and celery in front of a GCSE group. If I finished the class a couple of minutes early, I might just have time to catch Gurjit and a bite to eat before setting off for the work experience visit.

'I thought you'd follow me,' I said, running her to ground in the library.

'I had a class to go to, and it was obvious you might be some time. Have you come to any conclusions about the thefts?'

I shook my head. 'If you're determined to keep it completely hush-hush, then the only thing we can do is have me visit you on a night you'd normally be there. I can't make it tonight – I've got another visit. Tomorrow's Friday and—'

'I would be quite happy to work an extra shift,' she said.

'I sing on Friday evenings,' I said. 'In a choir. I can't let the other members down.'

That should convince her of the seriousness of my commitment. As it was, I don't suppose anyone would miss a back-row soprano, but I discovered an urgent desire to do something I actually wanted to do, rather than something I ought to be doing. We agreed to fix an appropriate evening soon. She seemed much calmer, as if sharing her anxiety had made it manageable; she even managed a smile. 'When you've sorted it out,' she said, 'it would give me great pleasure to invite you to a meal at my home.'

'That would be delightful,' I said, surprising myself by meaning it.

The staff room at fast. Picking up my lunchbox caused a little avalanche of paper. A couple of pieces of late homework. Richard's marking file – he must have put it down while he took a phone call. A query about a student's coursework. And a note from Ian Dale: would I phone him?

It took so long to get through the police switchboard I had started on my lunch, so I had to ask for him through a mouthful of celery. There was a message: he'd pick me up from college at five. There was something he'd like me to see.

Was there indeed?

I'd never before done such a perfunctory placement visit. But since the forecast threatened snow, and the whole city had the air of imminent disaster, everyone working with an eye on the darkening sky, doubtless the employers were relieved by my praiseworthy efficiency. In any case, everything seemed to be going according to the textbook, so my conscience was relatively clean.

Ian was waiting in the college car park when I got back. He sensibly suggested that we went via Harborne on the way to drop off my car.

'Via Harborne on the way to where?'

'Acocks Green, love. There's something you should take a look at.'

He wound his window up and started his engine before I could ask what; he enraged me further by grinning and tapping the side of his nose with his index finger. An impressive spurt of gravel, and he was gone.

Chapter Thirteen

A tedious rush-hour journey. Ian was waiting outside my house by the time I got there, and opened his passenger door before I could do more than think about dumping my bag of marking in the hall, so it had to join us in the car, where it huddled ignominiously between my feet. Ian sniffed, and put the car into gear.

'You'll have to tell me sooner or later,' I said.

'No. Not a word.' He drove in silence for a mile or more to prove his point.

I maintained an equal silence. Two could play at that game.

The first flakes of snow started to fall. Ian sighed. I sighed. He pulled up at last outside an unpretentious thirties semi, the sort of semi of which Acocks Green is made.

Karen's mother greeted us tearfully, but with the news that Karen had phoned to say she was all right, and would be in touch.

'Did you let WPC Green know?'

A nod. 'But I don't know where she is, you see.'

'Could you hear her clearly?' I asked.

'Well, she wouldn't be talking from the North Pole!'

I laughed, as if she had made a joke. 'But there might have been other noises, Mrs Harris. Traffic, or – or something.'

She shook her head.

'Well,' said Ian, 'if she does phone again, just see if you can pick up any background. WPC Green's got all the details of her money and bank account and so on? Good. Now, I was just wondering if I could have a quick look at her room again? I wondered if Sophie – you know, her college books . . .'

I would never have imagined Ian capable of such half-truths. Finding from somewhere a serious yet sympathetic smile, I followed him up the stairs before Mrs Harris could reply.

I would have thought, being Andy's cousin, that I'd seen him in most positions. I would have been profoundly mistaken. Codpiecing for Africa, hadn't he called it? There he was: pouty in tight jeans; out-Springsteening Springsteen; smiling sexily; languishing, ready for some teenager to come and save his life by taking him to bed. There must have been twenty-five or thirty sexy Andys, on doors, walls, wardrobes and even on the ceiling over the bed. A half-naked Andy would be the last thing Karen saw before she went to sleep at night and when she woke up in the morning.

'I thought you said she wasn't a fan,' said Ian, mildly.

'She told me it was her mum,' I breathed. One thing was clear: our little Karen was an accomplished liar. The posters went back about five years, though there were a couple of old ones – quite valuable if you happened to be a true devotee. 'This *is* Karen's room? Not her mum's?'

'Her mum's is quite an education as well. Tell you what – pretend to go to the bathroom and sneak a look.' Ian dropped his voice conspiratorially.

I raised my hands in mock horror and did as I was told.

I quite like the Bee Gees. OK, I like them a lot. I used to do my fitness routine to their greatest hits before I hit on the more silent Canadian Air Force exercises. But I didn't like them as much as Mrs Harris did, and I don't think I'd have thought of putting portraits of them together to make lampshades and a decorative firescreen. Well, I'd never have thought of making *anything* into a firescreen, to be honest. The only sign of reading matter was a pile of much-thumbed Bee Gees Fan Club newsletters on a bedside table.

There was a stirring down below: the return of Mr Harris, perhaps? While I used the loo, I pondered how he might deal with womenfolk so obsessed. Back to Ian: he'd laid a couple of William Murdock folders on the bed. Her timetable was stuck inside one of them.

'Why on earth didn't I think of it before? Asking her fellow students where she might be!'

Ian's face produced what might have passed as a smile. 'Even Stephenson's thought of that. But I have to admit, Sophie, she didn't get much out of them.' He coughed discreetly, and raised his eyebrow a millimetre: Ian, encouraging me to meddle? I could hardly believe it. 'Maybe someone else . . . No hurry, of course. But someone who actually knows the kids involved . . .'

'What a good idea, Ian,' I said. 'I wonder if there's anyone on the college staff who might help you?'

I was prowling round the room again. Poor Karen – she'd have died if she knew one of her teachers had invaded her privacy. A couple of blockbuster sex-and-shopping paperbacks; some teen magazines. I leafed through them idly – surely Karen was too old for these? And then I found one for slightly older girls, judging at least by the cover. I flicked it open idly. 'Remedies for Love.' What the hell – ?

It all seemed innocent enough, Herbs and spices. A little cayenne to make him hotter in bed; basil to sweeten his temper; and so on. It was just a silly, glossy magazine. But I wondered; might it be altogether more sinister? Karen had spent a lot of time in that kitchen at the Music Centre: what culinary arts might she have employed to make her man love her?

'Ian, we have to take this.' I held it up, pointing at the headline.

He came over, peering and then letting out a low whistle. 'Can't,' he said. 'Everything has to be done above board, remember?'

'Can't we ask Mrs Harris's permission?'

'Are we talking possible evidence here?' he demanded.

'Maybe only background.'

He wished I hadn't found it, didn't he?

An anxious Mrs Harris was waiting in the hall with a man whom she introduced as 'Mistrarris. Alan.'

He was a sweet-faced man, with round, rather prominent brown eyes and a smudge of a moustache inadequately concealing an upper lip bullied by the incisors it was supposed to conceal. His lower lip and chin did what they could, but sank chummily into the fold of his neck. He wore a honey coloured sweater and thick beige cords, stretched tight by his stomach.

We all shook hands.

'You'll find my little girl?'

His voice was surprisingly deep: I'd expected a whispering tenor.

'We're doing our best, sir,' Ian began, immensely kind. And then he stopped. I followed the line of his eyes. Mr Harris's side pocket was convulsing. He put his hand in, and removed it promptly, shaking it then putting the index finger in his mouth.

He shook his head; more in sorrow, it seemed, than anger. He turned to his wife. 'It's no good,' he said. 'There's no taming her.'

'A ferret,' Ian said. 'It's got to be a ferret.'

'Too big for a pocket. And there was no smell.'

'A clean ferret.' Ian had his head down on the steering wheel; tears of laughter glistened in the streetlights.

'No! You only have to look at him! A gerbil! I bet it's a gerbil!'

Had it been Chris, I could have inveigled him into letting me look at the magazine, once it had officially been logged in. But it wasn't Chris. So it was simpler to battle through the now vicious snow to the newsagents, which stayed open the most appalling hours, and try to buy my own copy. Fortunately they always had an heterogenous supply of reading matter, and they let me dig through old copies till I was filthy, stiff – and successful.

What I now needed was a tame pharmacist with patience, to tell me if any of the herbs in the so-called remedies might be toxic. There was an obvious candidate: Carl. If he could call me, I could call him. So I did.

As luck would have it, it was his wife who answered. I got a sub-zero reception when I asked to speak to him. There was, of course, no way she would do anything as simple as call him; she went – excessively slowly, it seemed at my end – to fetch him.

'Sophie? What do you want?' His tone was ultra-business-like. I thought I detected the click of another extension being lifted.

'Helleborin,' I said.

'I beg your pardon?'

I'd swear she echoed him.

'Could you tell me if any of the following plants contain helleborin?' I read out the list in the teen mag.

'Negative. But telling anyone to put anything in anyone's drink to change their behaviour is irresponsible in the extreme'. He sounded outraged. Did he think I was going to try it on him? 'One person's common herb may be another person's allergen. Even simple things like parsley!'

'Parsley?' I echoed. 'But that's supposed to be good for you!'

'A lot of things good for you in small amounts can be damaging if you take them in concentrated form,' he said. 'Parsley's one of them – the seed, in particular.'

'Oh. Anything on basil or mint?'

'Pennyroyal – is that on your list?'

'Yes. As a remedy for irregular periods.'

'They used to use it as an abortifacient.'

I was lost for words.

We exchanged a couple of polite sentences about the following week's trip and I hung up.

I ought to sit and think this through. If Karen had been inspired by this article to try and influence Andy – a big if, since I didn't think even she was that stupid – at least she'd only have put trivial, probably harmless, herbs and spices in his drink. But what if she'd been inspired – if that was the word – to experiment? That meant she had almost certainly been responsible for Pete Hughes's death. No wonder she was distressed. But what if she just *thought* she'd done him harm? – That would cause her at least as much misery. I ought to have read those letters. In fact, I ought to go into college and read them right now . . .

Chapter Fourteen

I woke up with a start, ready to run, my heart pounding, my hands tense. Why was I asleep at my dining-table? And then that didn't matter, because whatever had woken me hadn't been part of any dream.

There it was again!

Someone was at the front door, fiddling with the lock.

I froze.

Rationally, I knew I was quite safe. I had deadlocked the front door: no one could get in. The Yale lock rattled again. Then someone started on the Chubb.

I scuttled into the kitchen and reached into a cupboard. No one was going to get me without a struggle. I crept towards the hall, hiding behind the half-open kitchen door.

Another rattle: the Chubb lock responded, all five levers of it. The door opened.

'Sophie?'

'Andy! You stupid bastard!' I flung into the hall. 'You had me wetting myself with fear and you nearly got a faceful of this!'

'But I always let myself in. That's why you gave me the keys.'

'You always ring first.'

'I did!'

'You bloody well didn't.'

'I pressed the bell. Is it my fault if it doesn't ring? Your batteries must be flat: where's that tester gadget?'

'In the glory hole.' I flounced off to get it. And then I came back. 'What the hell am I doing, testing batteries?'

'Well, you need to know if your doorbell rings, don't you?'

Andy followed me to the kitchen table with the noise end of the bell. He prised off the back, and fished out the batteries: 'There. Flat as pancakes! Any spares?'

I pointed at the glory hole.

He reached in. 'They're your last ones. Where's your shopping list?' He scribbled on my kitchen jotter. 'What's the matter? And what the hell's *that*?'

'I told you, you scared me. And *this* is something Chris got for me to deal with unwelcome visitors.'

'Christ – is it CS gas?'

I patted the little canister. 'He didn't want to tell me and I don't want to know. He didn't lift it from police stores, don't worry. He brought it home from a conference in the States. Free sample.'

'OK, I don't need chapter and verse. Sit down before you fall down, why don't you?' He pulled a chair back for me and, when I sat, pressed my shoulders down. 'Jesus, that's some dose of stress you've got. What's up? Apart from thinking I'm Burglar Bill, that is.'

'Quite a lot,' I said. And gave him a brief resumé.

What I wanted him to do, of course, was give me the complete run-down on where he'd been, phone Ian and do the same, then deal with all the other problems. For once – just once – in our relationship, I wanted him to be grown-up and responsible. Just once would have been enough.

'So, is there any news about that kid?'

'None – and I – hell! I was going into college! Look, I'll see you in a bit – OK?' I was on my feet.

'Well, it would be, if you were going anywhere. But surely even your august seat of learning closes down for the night.'

'Of course – but—'

'And I'd imagine that it would be all tucked up by ten?'

'It's not ten o'clock!'

'No. It's eleven.'

I gazed at him. Then, as it dawned on me that he wasn't joking, I looked at all the little clocks on the kitchen appliances. They all agreed: one minute past eleven.

'Are you all right?' he said; he sounded anxious.

'Fine! Why?'

'You're sure? You're very pale. Look at you – you can hardly stand up.'

Come to think of it, sitting did seem altogether safer. I sat.

'Fancy a cup of – hell and damnation!' He fell over my bag of marking, which I'd dropped in its usual place: he picked it up in some irritation and looked inside. 'Why is your lunchbox still full – well, nearly full!' He waved a stick of celery at me, the marks of my teeth evidence that I'd had at least one bite. 'Some executive sweep you off to an expense-account lunch at the Mondiale? No? And what – since this kitchen is uncommonly tidy – did you have for supper? Sophie, kid, you really do run risks with your health. What shall I get you?' He washed his hands, dried them carefully, and dug in the fridge.

A bowl of pasta and a glass of wine later, I was feeling much better. But Andy clearly wasn't. He'd got that transparent look about the eye sockets that he always got when he was tired or stressed. Since it was now nearer midnight than I cared to think about, with a nine o'clock class to start my Friday, I could quite understand how he felt. I also knew that if I started to ask any questions he didn't like – and I knew he wouldn't like any of them – he'd go to bed faster than I could put out the milk bottles. But I had to mention Karen. It was still snowing, though not much had settled, and I was terribly afraid she might feel that sleeping rough was a heroic way to get Andy's attention. Or Andy.

'Did Karen strike you as . . . unusually smitten?' I asked.

He shrugged and pulled a face. 'Some of these girls – I'm not being politically incorrect, they're not women – they frighten me. They're virtually children, but they want real sex. Some go to lengths which – well, they disgust me. At first I wondered if the threats could possibly – but surely a teenage girl couldn't – could she?'

'What's Ruth say? She's had enough experience of the breed.' I suddenly realised I hadn't asked after her. 'I'm so sorry – is she any better?'

'Lots. I'm quite surprised, actually, because she left all her herbal remedies back in Devon. It must be the northern air. Look – I ought to phone her, and Griff told me not to use my mobile—'

It was easier just to nod permission than to ask why the hell he'd left it so late. Surely he should have called the minute he arrived: with luck she'd tell him so.

Closing the dishwasher door on the dirties, I reached down breakfast crockery. Whatever mode Andy was in at the moment, he'd have to put up with bread – or toast – and jam. There was nothing else in the breakfast line, despite the fact that the freezer was full of frozen curries and stews and a couple of exotic gateaux; I'd even polished off the spare bread I always kept handy. Somehow I'd have to fit in a supermarket shop, though Fridays weren't the best days for whizzing round the aisles.

'Right,' Andy said, putting his head round the door, 'early start. Six-fifty to Newcastle. OK for a lift?'

'Provided you'll dig me out of the drifts,' I said: weary or infuriated, I wasn't sure which.

'You're on. I'll wake you at six.'

I was so near an orgasm. So very near. But Kenji pulled away, and his funny monkey's face was replaced by Chris's, or at least what little of Chris's face I could see underneath his flat police cap.

'Out!' he yelled, and Kenji gathered up his thesis and waved goodbye. 'I've got a date with CNN anyway,' he said, over his shoulder.

Chris pulled his cap further over his eyes. He had a senior officer's baton and a failing erection.

And it was morning. And I was cold because the duvet had gone walkabout. No orgasm, either.

I was fully showered, dressed and made-up before I could bring Andy back to life.

'You'll have to move fast – there's quite a lot of snow.'

I threw him our communal dressing-gown; he grabbed it and was beside me at the window, staring down at Balden Road. Not even a milk float had sullied the snow. Next-door's cat had made it halfway down my path, before changing what passed in its case for a mind.

The roads weren't in fact too bad once we reached the bus routes, which had been salted and gritted. We made New Street Station rather more quickly than a normal traffic-filled morning, and I parked with no problems.

'I'm seeing you on to the train – no arguments.'

'I should be grateful,' he said, muted, and set off at a spanking pace to the booking hall.

It was only after he'd bought his ticket – second-class – that I was able to say it. 'I think you're taking the most enormous and totally unjustified risk. You should consider other people, even if you refuse to consider yourself. And – listen to me, don't turn away – you should have told the police where you were.'

'Guilty as charged,' he said roughly. 'Tell you what – as soon as you see the train pull out, you can call the fuzz and they can meet me at Newcastle.'

'That is, of course, if you're still on the train at Newcastle.' His face gave him away. 'What the hell are you up to, Andy?'

'Tell you when I can, love. You know that.'

'I don't. Not with you in this mood.'

'It's not a mood. Look, just give me a break, will you? I'll be happy to talk to the police – once I get back to Ruth.' He fished out his diary and scribbled. 'There – my address and phone number. I promise I'll go straight there and stay there until the police are happy. Or if they want me back in Brum I'll come back to you – if that's OK?'

I nodded, reluctantly.

'Phone the fuzz as soon as the train pulls out and give them that address. And then swallow it!' He grinned and hugged me. 'And find that kid – what's her name, Karen? – and persuade her to fall in love with a local lad. How about Andy Hunt? He's got nice knees, so Ruth tells me.'

'She's probably a Blues supporter,' I said, returning the hug.

Despite everyone's loudly-expressed fears that the train would no doubt be delayed by the wrong kind of snow, it pulled in on time. Andy got a seat and returned to the door, leaning out to talk to me.

'Andy,' I said, 'couldn't you give up Africa and play trains instead? You could be to rail travel what Richard Branson is to aeroplanes! Sorry, only joking.'

'I don't think rail privatisation's all that funny,' he said. But his expression was stony: I shouldn't have laughed about Africa.

A silence ballooned between us. I was frightened; we never used to have secrets. If we'd rowed, there was always a joke to bring us back together. But this wasn't a row; it was a withdrawal. At last, the guard started looking officious. And suddenly Andy flung open the door, stepped out and kissed me.

'It'll be all right, kid. I promise,' he whispered. He stepped back in, slammed the door, and was gone.

As soon as the train had disappeared, I set off to find a phone. Ian was up and about, but still at home. He read Andy's address and number back to me, to make sure he'd got it right. 'I'll get on to the transport police – make sure they keep an eye on things between here and the north. OK? And Sophie – there's a wine-tasting competition next weekend and I've entered you as my partner.'

The car was still wearing a thick layer of snow on its roof, but little rivulets were beginning to trickle pathetically down the windscreen and rearscreen. I got in, dodging drips, and sat down. Seven o'clock: what useful thing could I possibly do at seven? There was no point in going home, because with even the small amount of snow still left rush-hour would be truly vile this morning. I'd no idea what time Tesco opened, or college: not for a while, at any rate. The best thing to do was head for college and park. With a bit of luck I could be at Tesco for eight, stock up, and be in class for nine: a little miracle of organisation. To celebrate such inspiration, and to fill the silence, I reached in the glove box for a tape.

I was greeted by a wodge of brown spaghetti.

Breathing carefully, I picked it all out, checking each cassette as I did so. Beethoven Piano Sonatas – OK. Brahms Piano Concertos – OK. The Bee Gees – OK. Yuri Bashmet – OK. Andy Rivers's 'Raging' album – gutted. Completely gutted. That was the source of the spaghetti.

I gathered the whole lot in my hands and pressed it to

my eyes. I knew now where I'd better go: back to Harborne, to Rose Road Police Station. Andy might have a cavalier attitude to the police but just for once I was going to prove to Ian and Diane Stephenson and everyone else that I was on the side of the angels. Evidence that someone wanted Andy destroyed? Here it was, in my own hands.

Chapter Fifteen

'Are you seriously expecting me to believe that not only have you no idea *when* this was done, but that you have no idea *where* it was done?'

Perhaps Stephenson wasn't a woman for mornings. Perhaps I wasn't. One thing was for sure: between us we were making a pig's ear of communicating a simple fact. Ian worried a hang-nail; the silence in her office deepened.

'Look, Diane, would I joke about this? I'd give my back teeth to be able tell you when my car was broken into. And my front teeth. Apart from anything else, I feel *violated*. Someone's been in my territory, fingering my property.'

'Would you like me to refer you to Victim Support, Ms Rivers?'

I would dearly have liked to ram her neatly poised ballpoint down her long and elegant throat. What the hell was the matter with the woman?

'All I ask is that you believe me,' I said, very calmly. On my lap, my knuckles cracked. 'At no point have I ever suspected that my car has been interfered with. I've had no reason to. I always leave it locked, with one of those mechanical immobilisers on it. You can check for yourself that no one's smashed their way in. And I usually listen to the car radio if I want entertainment. I leave the car in the car park at work, or out on the road at home.'

'You have a perfectly good garage.'

'It's full of plants over-wintering at the moment.' I looked at Ian for confirmation, which came in the form of a cautious nod.

'OK, I suppose we shall have to accept that.' She leaned back in her chair, twiddling that bloody ballpoint.

'D'you want to fingerprint it?'

'Anyone professional enough to break into a car as unobtrusively as you allege would scarcely leave prints behind. But I'll get it done as soon as I can.'

'I'll ask one of the lads to drop it off at college for you, shall I?' Ian asked kindly, earning a cold glance from his boss.

I smiled back at Ian; when I spoke I found I hadn't managed to infuse the chill I'd intended into my voice. 'I might as well get off to work, then.' Gathering up my bag, I remembered a question I ought to have asked in the beginning. 'Is there any news of Karen Harris yet? And any response to those love potions from the forensic scientists?'

Ian shook his head. 'Give us a chance, love.'

'And Andy himself? What are you doing about him?'

'Bit of a law unto himself, isn't he?' said Ian. 'Bit cavalier, like.'

'A lot cavalier,' I agreed, my voice as dour as Ian's. 'And stupid with it. Travelling second-class, on a public train!'

'Nice and public, Sophie. More people around. Anyway, I've contacted the transport police, and he'll be met by more than Ruth at Newcastle. Besides which, I'd have thought one of Griff's mates would be somewhere around. He might be full of bravado—'

' – shit—' Stephenson amended.

' – but he's no fool. He's probably got a minder tucked away somewhere out of sight. Wouldn't be surprsied if he's put a tail on you to make sure you're safe.'

Stephenson slapped a file down hard on her desk. 'It'd do my heart good to think we could charge him with wasting police time.' Clearly she needed another dose of his charm.

'You never answered my question about Karen.'

'Ms Rivers, we have contacted all her college, school and other friends. All personnel are looking for her. She phoned her mother again, by the way, about half an hour ago.'

So where was she? 'I suppose the call couldn't be traced? No? She'd dialled whatever it is first?'

'141, yes.'

'Any identifiable background noises?' Silence. Wrong question. 'OK – I'd better be on my way.'

Neither thought it necessary to delay me. Thanks to the 103 I was scarcely late for work.

How I was supposed to combine teaching an Access group all morning and a GCSE group in the afternoon with the interrogation of the A-Level students which Ian had hinted at, I simply didn't know. All the lifts still being out, I made it to the eighth floor to pick up the register which I had to complete for my class – fifteenth floor – and would then have to return, collecting another for the afternoon's class – second floor. Richard was just unlocking his office as I staggered past to the administrator's room. The walk up had done him more harm than me – he was grey and gasping.

'Here, let me,' I said, grabbing the key and opening the door. 'Look, Richard,' I added, 'you've only got less than two months before you go. For God's sake make sure you live long enough to enjoy your retirement!'

I picked up his briefcase, and was ready to take his arm if necessary, but he waved me aside. 'Just out of condition,' he gasped. 'Haven't got your asthma spray, have you?'

Asthma? It looked more serious than that to me, but I wiped the mouthpiece of my salbutamol spray and passed it without a word. While his colour slowly came back, I found I was digging my nails into my hands. He had to be all right – *had* to be. It wouldn't be fair for him to—

But he was upright again, and smiling. 'Sorry about that. Tell you what, though – I could do with a cup of tea. If you could ask Florence?'

I made it myself.

Richard's suggestion was that I should give the Access group some written work for the second half of the morning, when he himself would be free to sit with them, enabling me to question Karen's friends. I baulked at the thought of him tackling even more stairs, but he anticipated my objections: he had a meeting on the thirteenth floor at lunch-time – we both had, hadn't we? – so he'd have to make it up there anyway.

'You could reconvene the meeting down here in your room,' I said.

'What? And inconvenience all those people?'

Each of the girls gathered – at Richard's suggestion – in the Conference Room was adamant: Karen had spoken of coriander.

To anyone else, coriander was just another herb or spice, a slightly exotic parsley or mint; but coriander was my *special* herb, the obsession I'd shared with my dead friend George. When he remembered, Andy would bring a pot for my window sill, and I would crush a leaf from time to time to bring out that lovely spring-green smell. Sometimes it made me cry. More often these days I'd smile at a memory of George, and be comforted.

'Why coriander, for goodness' sake?' I asked. Despite myself, I couldn't keep the asperity out of my voice. Any other herb she was welcome to . . .

'Because of this article. Out of her mind, if you ask me. That's why—'

'Why what, Farhana?

Farhana looked at her feet. I looked round the rest of the circle. 'Come on – what's up?'

Becky caught my eye briefly. 'She swore us to secrecy. So when the fuzz came sniffing – well, you see . . .'

'Rather than betray a confidence you kept your mouths shut. No problem. Except now she's been missing some thirty-six, forty hours.'

There was a tiny but distinct frisson: they all knew more than they were letting on. But something told me a frontal attack wouldn't work, at least not yet.

'Have any of you ever been to her home? Farhana?'

She flushed. 'It's my dad, Sophie. Won't let me – you see, she's not Muslim.' She touched her head-covering, as if to remind herself of something.

'Becky?' She'd be C of E if she was anything.

'Only the once. To pick her up.' She squirmed. 'It's her dad, see. Creepy.'

'*Creepy*?' The choice of word surprised me.

'That voice of his. And he smells. Like – like my gran's kitchen.' She dropped her voice and mouthed, 'Mice.'

Predictable giggling.

'Mind you,' Becky added, 'I don't reckon he's any worse than her mum. She's really flaky. Says she's psychic. And she says she can will parking spaces to appear – and she can, I've seen her do it.'

Clearly a useful skill.

'Crystal balls? Tarot?' I must have sounded too flippant. 'Have any of you ever seen the rest of the house? Her bedroom?'

Half a dozen heads – blonde, Afro and covered – shook solemnly.

'What about Karen? Does she believe in any of this? I'd have thought she was a bit too streetwise.'

'Nobody's streetwise when it comes to men,' said Becky.

'So what about blokes? Was she going out with anyone? Did she fancy anyone?'

Predictable giggles.

'I reckon she fancied this bloke she met at the Music Centre.' I shot at random, but by the surreptitious exchange of glances I reckoned I'd hit something. 'Did she tell you about him?'

Farhana shook her head. 'Muslims don't talk about such things in Ramadan.'

Not officially, maybe, but I was sure she was in on Karen's plans.

'*I* do! All the time!' Becky was starting to giggle. 'He fancied *her*, at least. She said he fell in love with her soon as he saw her.'

'You wouldn't have a name for this guy, would you?'

Damn! I'd gone too far.

'Don't want to get her into no trouble.' That was Soos, shaking her hair-extensions till the beads in them rattled. 'She goes, if her folks find out they'll go spare.'

'Set the mice on her,' Farhana said, and stopped, covering her mouth.

Some time I'd have to tell her it was all right to laugh. Even in Ramadan.

I was just locking the room when Soos came back. 'That coriander, Sophie.' She glanced around quickly – no, there was no one to overhear. 'It's to make him fancy her. It's an afro – afro-something—'

'Aphrodisiac?' I prompted, keeping my voice neutral, as if this were just an English vocabulary test.

She nodded. The beads rattled like bones.

If I listened very carefully I'd be able to hear someone saying it. Think about the voice. Not Brummie . . . Australian, that was it! Sam the chef, talking about the kid with the beautiful bum. He and Karen had something in common since they both . . . since they *both* came from Acocks Green. Where had my brain been?

The staff room was seething with students, and all the phones were in use, even the one on my desk. I dumped my bag on the heap of paper in what I hoped was an authoritative manner and looked ostentatiously from the phone to my watch and back again. Eventually the message penetrated my colleague's skull, and with ill grace she passed it across to me. Since she'd been talking to her mother in Scotland, possibly at William Murdock's expense, I didn't apologise for harrying her.

It took ten years to get through to Ian's extension – and then he wasn't there. Inspector Stephenson? Needs must, I supposed.

She greeted my theory without enthusiasm.

'Look, you have that list of roadies and other hangers-on. Wouldn't it be worth at least checking on that lad from Acocks Green? His address would be there, surely.'

'When I've got someone free.' Her voice dripped uninterest. Perhaps it was time to wake her up a bit.

'There is one other thing. Karen's friends think she might have put something in Andy's drink.'

'I beg your pardon?'

Damn it! Couldn't she show decent excitement, like a normal person?

'Apparently she spoke of coriander. I suppose the contents of the flask didn't include coriander?'

'Ms Rivers, you must realise I can't possibly give you that kind of information.'

'OK.' And I put the phone down. She wouldn't expect a courteous valediction and I was incapable of giving one.

The papers I needed for the lunch-time meeting were in my filing tray. By now I was five minutes late, a churlish response to Richard's generosity. I grabbed everything in the tray, realised I'd had no time to buy a sandwich, and scarpered.

We were deep into quality control systems, and I was shuffling through the papers which summarised a student survey about which Mags was supposed to be pontificating. She always liked intelligent questions, so I'd better invent one. Fast.

I know I said it aloud. 'My God! How stupid can I get?'

I expect everyone looked at me. They certainly did when I got to my feet, and rushed to the door. Richard's voice was frigid with anger: 'Sophie?'

'I'm sorry. I really am. But these are Karen's letters!'

The police would have to have them. But not until I'd read them.

I locked myself into a staff loo – at least no one would interrupt me there – and slipped the first from the envelope. It was a letter to someone else, of course, and I found unfolding the pages hard. Did I have the right to break Karen's confidence?

OK. Time to read it.

The letter itself was reasonably short: all the extra pages turned out to be poems she'd written to him. On the other hand, it was reasonably embarrassing, and I could quite understand why she hadn't wanted Andy to see it. Apart from a complete run-down on how he made her feel – vaginal lubrications included – she quoted at length and not always accurately from his songs. Oh dear. Letter two was shorter, more conventional, and included a couple of lines which alarmed me:

Truly I would rather die than hurt you, or even think about hurting you, you do understand don't you that I'd rather die. I realise now I made a mistake, and only hope you will forgive me.

If only they had phones in lavatories. And then I discovered I didn't want Stephenson to know about this. Not yet. Maybe, just maybe, there was some other explanation for Karen's verbal excesses, and Stephenson appeared to have the most literal of minds.

It dawned on me at long last that there might be more than one way of skinning a cat. OK, Stephenson wouldn't tell me Acocks Green Man's address – but Ollie would know the address of the caterers for whom he'd been working. From there to running the young man to earth might take for ever – but at least it was a start.

Chapter Sixteen

I suppose I should have expected it. Ollie had switched off his mobile phone. Even though I knew it was useless I tried him on his home number. Unobtainable: he'd no doubt forgotten to pay the bill again.

I stared around the emptying staff room hoping for inspiration. I was late for class again, but I had other priorities. Phone Missing Persons and give an anonymous tip-off? But Karen had probably gone quite voluntarily, and might well be staying quite voluntarily. Might *not* be. Theory's one thing, practice another.

Cursing my good citizenship, I dialled Ian's Rose Road number: please let it be Ian, not Stephenson to answer it. *Please.*

'I'm sorry – there's no reply from that extension. Can anyone else help you?'

Exasperated, yet at bottom relieved, I left a message asking Ian to call me asap. And promising myself I'd make more time at break, I went off to teach.

Break found the Rose Road number constantly engaged. Ollie's phone was still switched off. And someone had left the Yellow Pages on my desk, open at 'Estate Agents'. It didn't take very long to turn it to 'Caterers'. OK, so I couldn't remember what they were called: seeing the name in print might just jog my memory. *Might.*

Vineyard Caterers? Something to do with booze?

Mags popped in, distributing the Union newsletter.

'What's the latest?' I asked, wondering if it was worth my time to read it.

'Jungle drums are reporting redundancies at George Muntz,' she said. 'That's where you were, wasn't it?'

I nodded. And slapped my head. Grapevine! That's what it was. And my finger was tapping the digits before I could work out why I'd thought of it. And before I'd thought of a plausible cover-story.

My mother would have described as cultured the voice which answered. I said the first thing that occurred to me – that I was wondering about work experience placements.

'Oh, I shouldn't think so. We're a very small organisation.'

Infusing a benign glow of innocence into my voice, I jumped in before she could cut me off. 'But you do some very prestigious events, don't you?'

'Well—'

'Didn't you do that wonderful spread at the Music Centre the other night? Saturday?'

'That's it, you see – we have to maintain our standards.'

'Are all your staff specially trained, then? Or do you use temps?'

'Even the temporary staff are trained silver service waiters.'

Great. I was getting precisely nowhere, and irritating her to boot.

'Ah,' I said, playing for time, 'that explains their professionalism. In fact,' I added, growing ever more inventive, 'I was speaking to one of your young men on Saturday, at the Music Centre Reception, about the possibility of his doing further training. I promised him some information about part-time courses. But I can't remember his name, only that he lived in Acocks Green.'

'*Acocks Green*? In that case, Miss Er – I don't think I'm able to help you. We only take on staff from – er—'

The better suburbs, no doubt. God, what snobs! And wasn't that outright discrimination?

She realised what she'd said. 'The travel, you know. Acocks Green is rather – remote. Good after—'

'Oh, but he was very well-spoken. Public school, I think he mentioned.' God forgive me! 'Very tall, very well turned-out. A credit to you. And I feel *so* bad about letting him down—'

'Let me think – it could be – I'm afraid I simply can't divulge names over the telephone, Miss Er – it would be entirely irresponsible. If you care to leave the materials you spoke of at my office I would be happy to pass them on. The Olton office.'

Hell – miles away. Quick! 'Do you do most of your work that side of the city?'

'Indeed no. This evening, in fact, we shall be catering at the Cem – I really don't know why you're asking all these questions. Good afternoon.'

Win some, lose some. *The Cem* – It couldn't be the Cemetery, could it. Come on, Sophie. *The Cem* – No. Nothing. No further forward – *and* late for class.

All the snow had disappeared in the course of the day: there was even a hint of premature spring in the air. Time to go home. Sure enough, my Renault sat patiently in the car park. Remembering why the police had been looking after it for me, I approached it quite gingerly. It seemed all right. I'd seen people on TV looking under their cars: I'd look too, even if I wasn't sure what for.

Returning to the vertical I found Richard peering at me.

'Exhaust,' I said.

'Well, it *is* Friday,' he said. And got into his Volvo and reversed out.

Friday. Freya's day. Come to that, Thor's day and Woden's day. And there's that Black Country town, Wednesbury, to which radio announcers allocate four distinct syllables while we all pronounce it Wensbry. I was well into the Monument Road traffic jam for the Ivy Bush intersection with Hagley Road, cheering myself with musings about mispronunciations, when it struck. What if, by all that was wonderful, Catering Woman hadn't said 'Cem—' but 'Cen—' and she was talking about the Centennial Centre? Half a mile from here. Less. And I was a few cars short of the one-way system. Signalling, belatedly, I wrenched the car round into one of the side roads and wriggled it round to face the opposite direction. I was on my way.

Parking was easy. Slotting into a place marked 'Reserved', I locked up and prepared to march in. Except it wouldn't be as simple as that. Security was sensible everywhere these days, and I didn't want to have to try Catering Woman's patience with any more specious explanations.

They say the devil looks after his own. At this point a little Rascal drew up: a delivery of flowers. They were cutting it a bit late if the function was this evening. And only one young woman to wrestle all those pretty table posies into the hall! Perhaps it would be polite to offer . . .

As I debated the risk, the woman disappeared inside, reappearing almost immediately with a tall young man wearing a white chef's jacket. I looked more closely. The young woman was an ex-William Murdock student. That was it – her parents had wanted her to take a degree, but she'd managed to get a temporary job in a florist's. At first she'd planned simply to take a year out, but she ended up enjoying her work so much she'd thrown up Uni altogether to manage a new branch of the florist's: 'Fleur's', tritely enough. And she – she was – Roberta? Some bad female adaptation of a male name – always reminded me of a lip-salve, or a disease. That was it! Nigella.

I approached slowly. It was dark, after all, and I had to be sure. But the gods were definitely on my side.

'Hey! Sophie, what are you doing here? Haven't seen you for ages! How are you doing? Oh, hell—'

One of the posies slipped out of the shallow cardboard box: I fielded it.

'Well held!' A male voice. And the voice came with enormously long legs and chef's trousers.

It didn't take the three of us long to carry in the remaining boxes; it was natural that I should help Nigella distribute the posies on the tables. But it was equally natural for Longlegs to back out and return to the kitchen – as he was now doing.

'Excuse me,' I said, sounding horribly like Joyce Grenfell, 'but haven't I seen you . . .' No, it was too crass. I sounded as if I were trying to pick him up.

He stopped, and looked back at me. 'Yeah, weren't you at the Music Centre? The main act's sister, or something?'

'Cousin. And – I'm sorry, I don't know your name—'

'Ford.'

'Ford – any chance of a quick word?'

He shrugged but, deciding it was best to humour the senile, motioned with his head to the door nearest to the kitchens.

'Well?'

'Look, Ford – I'm looking for someone. A student of mine.'

For a moment he stared, and then, hearing a movement behind him, turned. 'Not Karen, by any chance?' he asked.

And there she was, decked out in the neat Grapevine waitress's uniform.

Irresponsible was the most restrained of the words I could find to describe her, but there was no point in using it. She was seventeen, above the age of consent, and he was eighteen, so no legal blame could be attached to either of them. There was something touching – or nauseating – in the way they kept their hands on each other as they talked: his thumb slotted into her waistband, her hand cupping his right buttock. The sad thing was, of course, that the romantic idyll would have to be interrupted. The police and her parents needed to know the truth and they'd have to face, at the very least, recriminations. For though I hadn't spelt it out to Ian, I'd bet my next summer holiday that he'd deduced Karen had some plans in mind for Andy's drink, and I was equally sure that Diane Stephenson wouldn't forget my questions about coriander.

Which reminded me.

'Karen,' I said, interrupting the flow of their protestations of mutual love, 'I have to talk to you. OK, Ford?'

'OK. I should be back in there anyway.' He kissed Karen lingeringly on the lips and pushed back into the kitchen.

'What's *up*?'

'It's about Andy—'

'You've *never* been and shown him my letters!'

I shook my head. 'More serious than that. Karen – did you put anything in that flask of his?' I was appalled with myself. What had happened to tact? Or even commonsense?

But she was flushing. Not with righteous anger, but with guilt. She hung her head like a five-year-old.

'Well?' I tried to make my voice gentle.

'I wanted him to – you know. Fancy me. And there was a piece in this magazine talked about it. And Mum's always on about making things happen if you really want them to – I mean, she was in the same shop as Robin Gibb one day, so it only goes to show. So I looked in the library and I found this book and it said coriander was an aphrodisiac. But then there was a jar of it in the kitchen: Mum's got a lot of herbs she never uses. And I thought, if I could get it into one of his flasks – you know he has a supply made up and keeps one on stage – then maybe I could get off with him at the party. But then, when I'd done it – put the coriander in – this Australian guy reckons he doesn't have any special order for his flasks, so he could just as easily drink mine first as last, and fall in love with someone else.'

'I don't think aphrodisiacs work quite like that,' I said. 'How much coriander did you use? Was it seeds, or dried leaves?'

'Just said "powdered". About this much, I suppose.' She held her thumb and forefinger about an eighth of an inch apart. 'Between two *flasks*? Oh, Sophie! You're not saying – it hasn't done him any harm, has it? Made him ill? He wasn't allergic – oh, my God!'

'No, no! Calm down. No, Andy's perfectly all right. Perfectly.' I bit back all the things I wanted to say about her stupidity; they'd come soon enough from the police. I didn't see Diane Stephenson accepting the story as phlegmatically as I had. 'Look, you have to go and phone home. And tell them you're going home tonight.'

Her eyes flared. 'Not to stay! We're – we're – I want to stay with *Ford*?'

'Take him as well,' I said, suddenly tired.

Chapter Seventeen

There was no point in going home: choir practice started at seven-thirty. There was just time to fight my way through the Five Ways traffic jam and into Tesco's; who knows there might even be a sandwich left, or a healthyish snack. Right now I'd murder for a Kit-Kat, or some of those wonderful Belgian chocolates ready to leap into my trolley . . . Come on, Sophie – it's serious-shop time. Loo rolls; kitchen towels; tights; muesli; tea: I'd prise myself out of bed good and early tomorrow and cycle down to the butcher's and the deli in Lonsdale Road to get the more interesting things. Select the shortest checkout queue. Pray the bags don't tear. Back to the car park, shopping in the back seat, and off to the redundant church hall where choir practice would start in five minutes.

I'd failed to buy both the forbidden chocolate and a more sober sandwich, but managed to cadge some biscuits set aside for out mid-evening break. And then into Brahms's *German Requiem*.

I knew it like the back of my hand. I could go on automatic pilot.

One could always rely on Luigi to find food. Indeed, he prided himself on being able to provide spectacular snacks, so it made sense to go back with the others to The Duke of Clarence. I wouldn't drink, of course, not even after one of his wonderful baguettes: Maria's, more accurately, full of genuine Italian sausage and vegetables she always appeared to have picked from a non-existent garden just before trapping them in new bread. Yes, one of Maria's rolls: the thought of it kept me going, despite the rather pedestrian pace our choral director had for some reason chosen.

Into the night air at last. Give a lift to a couple of other sopranos. Park with some determination. Sweep into the bar. To find Jess (Brum for Guiseppe) in charge, his parents having flown out to Parma to a family funeral. No food. Not so much as a packet of crisps. To be sociable, I drank a glass of mineral water, and then excused myself. At the last moment, Mo, one of the sopranos, changed her mind and wanted a lift home. Good job I had someone with me, really. Because when I saw what was inside my car, I keeled right over.

I came to in what proved to be the family's room above the bar at The Duke of Clarence. I worked that out from all the photographs: Luigi and Maria; Luigi and Jess; Maria and Jess; Luigi and Maria and Jess. All of them, individually and collectively, along with Jasper the dog and his illustrious predecessors. And there was Mo, leaning over me with concern in every angle of her body. What I couldn't understand was why my eyes should be streaming and my nose on fire. Smelling salts? There was only one person I knew who carried smelling salts . . .

A finger touched my cheek: tentatively, I'd say, rather than tenderly.

'Sophie?'

'Chris! Thought you were down south.'

'I was. Thought I'd come back up for the weekend. Thought I might find you here. Not out cold, though.'

Struggling to the vertical, I smeared away some smelling-salt tears. 'Hungry, that's all.' And then I saw his face. '*Nearly* all.'

'Tell me,' he said.

A glass of milk appeared from somewhere. And some sliced supermarket white bread.

'Jess'll have to get rid of the evidence before his parents get home,' I said. 'But the butter's fresh.'

'So I should hope,' Chris said, 'and so were the flowers on that wreath.'

While my mouth was telling him all that had been going on, my brain was worrying about getting my car back, either to Harborne – or to Chris's house in Edgbaston. I knew he wouldn't want me to drive, although I was beginning to feel much better. Come to think of it, now I swung my feet to the floor – who'd have thought Maria and Luigi could be guilty of such a carpet? – I really didn't feel like driving. It would in any case mean having to decide where I was going.

At last, with Jess trying not to hover over me to hint that it was very late and I was wearing thin his hospitality, I rounded off the story. I realised Mo had gone: she'd have had to bum a lift from someone else. 'Which car shall we leave here?' I asked baldly.

'Neither. I'm having yours taken back to Rose Road, to let the Forensic Science team give it a valeting. You never know what they'll find. I'll take you back to your place – or mine. Whichever is more convenient.' So he didn't want to make a decision either.

'All my shopping's in my car,' I said.

He looked grave. 'Nothing's in your car. Nothing at all.'

He was exaggerating, of course. But when I saw my little Renault at Rose Road Police Station the following morning, I was glad he'd let me believe that my shopping had been stolen. The loo rolls and kitchen towels had been shredded, as if a giant gerbil had been at work; tea was scattered everywhere; muesli ditto. They'd left me my marking, but had soaked it in red ink. My tapes were still intact, but Chris told me they'd been wiped, probably with a magnet.

And the tights? It suddenly occurred to me that he'd not mentioned the tights.

Back in his office, he leaned across his desk, like a doctor about to impart news of a terminal illness.

'I was hoping you wouldn't ask,' he said grimly. 'Someone's – cut pieces out of them.'

'Any pieces in particular?'

A pause.

'The crotch. And then – they've been tied into a bow, round the wreath.'

I nodded: I supposed it was to be expected. 'The wreath. Did it come with a card?' I should have asked before. 'What was on the card?'

'A valediction to Andy Rivers. I gather from Diane Stephenson it's not the first. Sophie, what on earth have you said to put her back up? I've never known her like this – she's like a demented porcupine.'

'Could it be anxiety? That now she's done half the work, you're going to muscle in and take all the glory?'

'Which I assure you I'm not. It's her case – I'm back on the course on Monday. And I didn't get the impression it was me she resented – OK, I would say that, wouldn't I? But Ian's not happy about the situation between you—'

'To what – rather, to whom – does he attribute it?' It was typical of Chris to assume it was my fault we didn't get on; my anger was demanding an outlet.

'Oh, you know what he's like with younger officers.'

'No, I don't. I've never seen him anything other than supportive where you're concerned. But then, you treat him like a human being.'

His face closed.

How dared he back this incompetent young woman against Ian and myself! Damn it, we were still supposed to be lovers, though the emphasis after last night was definitely on the word, "supposed'. Yes, we'd shared a bed – at my house, on the grounds that my central-heating was on and the bed made up. But he had been so solicitous about my 'exhaustion' – when was I ever too exhausted for a nice bonk? – that it was clear he at least was not in the mood. He never was a man for protracted cuddles, and I wasn't surprised when he presented a cold back, which he didn't want warmed. He had been up and pyjama'ed by the time I surfaced, wearing his own dressing-gown.

I looked at his neatly organised desk and found I was shaking – with rage, with humiliation, with rejection. I wanted to hurt him, but I couldn't deny a lurking belief that if anyone were to get to the bottom of the threats against, the attacks on, Andy, it would be Chris. Deep-breath time.

'Any idea when I'll be able to have my car back?'

'Monday or Tuesday, I should think.' His voice was off-hand.

'Oh.'

'Is that a problem?'

'Well – being without your wheels—'

'You managed well enough without a car for years! I seem to remember urging you times without number to get one and you always found an excuse not to.'

'I seem to have developed petrol feet over the last few months. And I need one for my new job.'

If that was meant as a conversational lifeline, it didn't work. 'You'll have to take taxis for a bit, won't you? And you can't possibly regard your car as a safe means of transport. Bit of a liability, I'd have thought.' He managed a smile at last, but it was ironic.

I shrugged. Perhaps the view from the window would inspire me.

'How's Karen's mum?'

'I've not even looked at the file, Sophie.'

Plainly, it hadn't.

'Of course. But when you've had a chance to talk to people, perhaps you'd give me a buzz. Or perhaps you could ask Ian to—'

'See what I can do.' He stood up; the interview was at an end.

It was hardly worth catching a bus back from Harborne to Balden Road, but I regretted the bulky carrier bags: replacement tapes; tights from Boots, since for some inexplicable reason Safeway had stopped producing small thick tights; muesli; loo rolls; kitchen towels. The delicatessen provided deliquescent and delectable St Agur and some Cornish Yarg, and an organic loaf so solid you could have used it as a house-brick. Salad. Meat? Would Chris expect to eat his Sunday lunch with me, as he usually did when he was in Birmingham? Steak or chicken? Perhaps, I was just too tired to care.

When I got home, my fingers cut deep by the polythene carrier handles, there were no messages on my answering machine. Not one. No post either. And it was starting to snow. Perhaps what I needed to do was go into town and exercise my Barclaycard: how would Rackhams rate for personal safety? And then it occurred to me, like a blow to my stomach, that, apart from his disparaging remark about my car, Chris had made no mention of protecting me. Times they were a-changing, indeed.

It was weird, using Ian as a source of information. But if Chris hadn't known about Karen and Ford, then Ian would, and he might be cajoled into spilling enough information. However, it was Stephenson who took the call.

'Ms Rivers? I hope you're recovered from your experience last night. Most unfortunate.'

'I didn't make it any better by skipping lunch,' I said.

'Funny how crises always erupt when you unwrap a sandwich,' she said. 'And then – the indigestion!'

Anyone else and I'd have thought we were having a conversation.

'I find bicarbonate of soda helps,' she said.

Perhaps we were.

'Bicarb? How?'

'About an eighth of a teaspoon in warm water. Not hot. Shifts the wind.'

'I'll remember that. Look, I hope you don't mind my asking – ' I too can be conciliatory – 'but I was wondering how Karen got on last night.'

'Christ on a fucking bike! Talk about love's young dream! I tell you, it would have saved us a lot of trouble if she'd met Ford Scott before last Saturday.'

'You believe her?'

'Let's just say we've eliminated her from our enquiries. For the time being.'

'Thank goodness for that.' I was almost warming to the woman.

'So now we'll be looking more closely, I'm afraid, at Mr Rivers himself.'

Deciding that the snow really meant it, I gave up the idea

of a shopathon. I would do homely things like washing and ironing: securely bolted in, that is. And I would call Griff to find out what was happening to Andy, and, with a bit of luck, persuade him to get Andy to call me. A natter would be nice. Except there were all those things we couldn't talk about, lest we be overheard.

In the event, there was a bonus. The snow stopped, and I had a call from Shahida: would I like to eat with them and help bath Maria? I would. And to put gilt on the gingerbread Shahida's minicab driver brother-in-law would collect me and bring me home.

Made-up, and wearing something elegant but childproof, I felt much better. I knew from experience that Arun's sense of punctuality was poetic, so didn't worry when he didn't arrive promptly. In fact, I could make good use of the time.

Ollie. And by some miracle, his phone was switched on.

He never was much of a man for preliminaries. 'Sophie? Look, I'm working. Gig at the NEC.

'It's about Andy's gig, actually,' I said.

'Bad business. And the fuzz keep shoving their noses in – give them their due, they never stop – but they're no further forrarder.'

At least the shoving was good news.

'No further at all?'

'No. They come and hassle decent working men, but you can tell they're in the dark. Nice bit of skirt – sorry, Sophie – in charge though. I could fancy her. And Phiz is really smitten.'

'Surprise, surprise.'

'The lads are running a book on how long it takes him to get his hands in her knickers.'

'Well, they would. Tell me, is it the same team as the Music Centre gig?'

'More or less. Why?'

'I fancy doing a bit of poking around on my own account. After all, it was my cousin they were after.'

'Not what young Diane says. She'd like to nail Andy, if you ask me. Said something about bringing him to Brum for questioning – hello? Sorry, Sophie. Someone I need to talk to.'

'OK. I'll be as quick as I can. It's not just that they're after the wrong person – it means the right one could go unpunished. And that person's still at large.' I remembered my car, but thought better of telling him. 'Any remote chance you could let me have a list of the lads involved in Andy's gig? After all, you must have prepared one for the fuzz.'

'Should be able to put my hand on one for you. Why not have a pub lunch with me tomorrow and I'll give it you then? Give me a bell, twelvish? See you, darling!'

A blessedly efficient man, Ollie. His filing system was so neat and efficient even Chris would have found it a home from home.

A peremptory ring announced the arrival of Arun.

'I'm sorry to bring you out on a night like this,' I said.

'Working anyway. And it's nothing like Afghanistan. Man, you should see the snow there! That's what I *call* snow. This – this isn't worthy of the name.'

Looked at it like that, I supposed it wasn't.

'How's Fozia? She must be near her time.'

'Pretty big! Tell you what, Sophie, I'll be glad when it's all over. Funny thing,' he said, dropping his voice sheepishly, 'I've got beyond wanting it to be a boy. I mean, it'd be nice, and all that, but I just want to – you know, have her all right again.'

'Of course. No more thoughts,' I added, not very kindly, 'of going out to fight?'

'Kabul's no place for a family man.'

'Absolutely. So now what?'

A ruminative silence.

'Well,' he admitted, 'you know Shahida's always on at me to get my qualifications. Not that she should be working, not now she's a mother. Her place is at home.'

I didn't bite.

'So I thought I might do something at night school, like. Get some GCSEs.'

Thank goodness for that! I'd always hoped the idea of freedom fighting for Islam might pall. Arun was a bright young man – nearly as bright as his wife, whom I'd taught years ago. He'd been bored for years: perhaps fatherhood and study would be the twin answer.

What Shahida hadn't told me was that she was match-making again. I was all ready to don the PVC apron which is mine at bath-time when this delectable young man with almond-shaped eyes came into the living room. He was about five foot six – not that you look for height when you're only five foot one – and about my age. Afzal. A solicitor. So what was such a man doing unmarried, especially when it seems to be the ambition of every Muslim family I know to marry both sons and daughters off when they're hardly into their twenties?

I'm not generally keen on being paired off, even by my friends. But you never know when you'll need a solicitor, so I prepared to charm and be charming. And thus passed a delightful evening.

Arun appeared promptly at eleven. It seemed that working parents needed early nights. And Afzal and I went our separate ways.

Chapter Eighteen

I wish I'd been that owl, watching from the sycamore tree opposite.

He'd have witnessed a small woman, insistent that she didn't need any help to get out of a D-registered blue Datsun; and a tall, broad-shouldered Asian man, driver of the car, equally insistent that she did. And as she struggled out, he seized her by the arm.

OK. Tame so far. But then another man rushed up, scrabbling for a grip on the icy pavement, and cannoned into the others, knocking them both off their feet. The Asian was quicker to recover. Soon on his feet, he was braced for unarmed combat: braced until he fell over. Each time the woman made an effort to join him in an upright position, she was knocked back down by a flying male foot. Soon, all three were in a sprawling heap. What a pity they weren't voles, or rats! They'd have been easy pickings.

'*No*! Stop it, the pair of you! Here, pick me up.' I stuck up my arms. 'Chris, this is Arun: Arun, this is the police. The *police*!'

Arun was first on his feet, having crawled off the path and on to the grass. He leaned over to me, but by now Chris was vertical enough to want to help. So an ungainly procession staggered to the house: end of owl's entertainment.

And at this point I got frightened.

I always drew my living-room curtains and left on the lights: elementary burglar precautions. Sometimes I left the radio on a talk programme though I couldn't remember doing so this time. But this didn't sound like a radio voice. It sounded like someone having a row. In my living room.

The door at least was undamaged, so whoever had got in had done so with a key. Chris's was poised in his hand; so was mine. Cocking an eye at Chris, who nodded sternly to Arun, I inserted it. The men shouldered their way in, the senior policeman and the Afghan warrior. I followed.

He was no match for them, of course. They brought him down easily, but not before he'd unloosed a stream of invective that startled even me.

'Andy? What the hell d'you think you're doing? Chris – Arun – this is my cousin Andy.'

Chris extended a disdainful hand; Arun stood by, suspicious, then extended his in turn.

'You all right now, Sophie? You just call me if you have any hassle – right?'

'Right. Thanks very much, Arun. Sorry for all this – trouble. And thanks for making the evening so splendid.' I saw him to the door.

It took no more than a couple of minutes to wave him off. Then I came in, via the kitchen, to poke the central-heating into another hour's life. I filled the kettle and fished out the Jameson's – each to his own. I took the whiskey and three glasses through: anyone wanting coffee could make it.

'Sophie, what the hell are you doing out at this time of night?'

Had they had time to rehearse it: this simultaneous interrogation? I shrugged, being deliberately obtuse. 'It's only just gone eleven.'

'You know what I mean,' said Andy.

'And with *that* guy? Drugs have been wanting to nail him as long as I can remember. Jesus, Sophie—'

'You sound just like Ian Dale,' I said.

'Why didn't you tell me where you were going?' he continued, as if I hadn't spoken.

'You moan at me for not taking care of myself,' Andy chimed in, 'and then you go out with that bastard! Your latest bit of rough, is he? Chris, can't you get some sense into her?'

'Gave up trying. What the fuck are you doing here, anyway? I thought you were safely down at Rose Road.'

'I told Stephenson where I'd be staying. She didn't object – in fact, she had me delivered here, and a couple of kids checked the place over to make sure it was safe. Don't see how she *could* object, anyway – I'm not under arrest. I've co-operated fully, my stuff has been searched, I've even handed over my keys so they can search my home. They've already given what was supposed to be a safe house the spring-cleaning of its life. I did offer them my passport, but I had to change my mind about that – I'm due at the White House next Saturday.'

Did he *really* say that? Or had I imagined it?

I poured a couple of fingers' worth of Jameson's for myself, and waved the bottle at the other glasses. Both men nodded absently, but two hands reached eagerly for the tots when I'd poured them.

'So what are you doing here?' Andy made the question less offensive than it could have been.

'Trying to keep an eye on Sophie, of course. So where the hell *were* you?' Chris turned to me. 'I tried phoning you,' he said, thoroughly aggrieved.

'Out for supper at Shahida's. Wonderful meal.' Oddly, though, my stomach was protesting; since I was always on excellent terms with it, I didn't know how to react. With contempt, I decided, and swigged the Jameson's. I did, however, sit down.

'Sophie? Sophie?' The chorus effect would have made me laugh if I hadn't been fending off a spear of pain.

'Spot of indigestion, that's all,' I gasped. That was *all*? I hadn't so much as a peppermint in the house to ease it.

'Whiskey should be good for that,' Chris said anxiously. 'Shouldn't it?'

'Perhaps brandy instead? In the cupboard, chick?'

'Add some water – she usually sloshes it down neat.'

Had it not been for the pain, which doubled me up if I sat anything other than bolt-upright, I could have found the whole business entertaining. Andy went rooting round my kitchen, and then headed upstairs; he came back clutching a packet of antacid tablets. 'Corn in Egypt,' he said, passing one to me. 'Had a spot of bother in Canberra. These worked. Don't half make you fart, though.'

Chris inspected them. 'I can get some more from the rota chemist tomorrow.'

'Today,' I said, swallowing gungy peppermint and begging it to work.

'Have you got a hot-water bottle? That might help. Ruth swears by hot bottles.'

Revolted, I stood up. 'Never needed one. Night, night. Finish my whiskey, someone.'

So I had a police escort after all. At bed-time it was my stomach's fault we didn't bonk: next morning Chris was up harrying duty pharmacists before I even woke.

As days of rest went, Sunday wasn't very restful. After their initial bonding, Andy and Chris rapidly came unstuck. The process began with the news, accelerated with 'Letter from America' and was full-blown by the time we discussed lunch. Andy was in awkward though not vegetarian mode again, and was loudly unhappy about eating beef in the form of steak from my freezer. Chris cited government advice, and eventually I threatened to send Andy off on my bike to inspect the ORGANIC sign in Brown's window for himself.

Chris, full of conscious virtue, peeled and sliced potatoes.

What I couldn't understand was why Chris was hanging on. And on. What on earth was he getting from our relationship – if that was what it still was?

And then I remembered Ollie. We were supposed to be lunching! So how would the four of us get on? My stomach kicked at the thought of it. What I would dearly have liked to do was simply go on my own, leaving Andy and Chris to fight it out; I had, after all, a very strong suspicion that Chris would disapprove of the list I hoped Ollie was finding for me. And, as I chomped another antacid, I wondered what on earth I'd wanted the list for anyway. Why couldn't I leave well alone?

In the end, we all four sat down to a variety of roasts – nut roast for Andy – in a carvery that purported to be posh and specialised in cleverly-disguised cardboard. Chris, spare to the point of asceticism, tried not to sneer at Ollie's encroaching paunchiness and silly curly hair, while doubtless fulfilling the worst of Ollie's expectations of what a policeman should look like. Andy was in bland host mode. It was all very dull and depressing.

Ollie slipped me the list when – eventually – Chris went to the loo. 'God, that man's bladder capacity,' he muttered. 'There! Put it in your handbag, love. Hey, Andy, remember that time we doctored that geezer's handbag?'

'Supporting act,' said Andy, in parenthesis. 'Bloke had a handbag before they were commonplace. Some of the lads thought it would be funny to fill it with condoms.'

'Not what you lot'd call politically correct, of course,' Ollie chuckled. 'Close your bag, sweetheart – Laughing Laddie's on his way. Bags it isn't me tells him his flies are undone. Now, drink up, Sophie: *A glass of wine for your stomach's sake.* That's what it says in the Good Book.'

White wine couldn't do any harm. Could it? One sip and a red-hot poker plunged neatly into the place the whiskey had found last night. This was no longer in the least entertaining.

I've never played chess with anyone older than five, though I do have a very impressive set, which I keep as an ornament. I'd never have expected it to be a life-saver. Chris and Andy fell on it, pushing all my rubbish to the end of the dining table to make space for their confrontation: my preparation and I were relegated to the sofa. Since they appeared to be vying with each other to see who would take the longest time over each move, I judged it safe to examine Ollie's list. I knew one or two of the people, of course, including Phiz, but in general they were just names. Ollie had also listed nicknames and the field each man specialised in: sound, lighting, general dog'sbodying. And addresses and contact numbers – home and mobile. All very clear – and no use at all.

Silence from the chess-players.

At seven Andy broke it. 'If you've got a bad stomach, chick, you should eat something.'

Before I had time to be touched by his thoughtfulness, he added, 'And Chris and I could manage a sandwich.'

At nine, Chris pushed away from the board. 'Shit! I'm going to have to concede. I should have been on the road hours ago. Back to the grindstone.'

He lingered long enough to use the lavatory and pick up his bag – I later found yesterday's socks, pants and shirt his side of the bed – and was off. A warm handshake for Andy. A distant peck on the cheek for me.

Andy returned to the board, reliving the moves he and Chris had made. 'You know, he shouldn't have conceded.' He muttered something about rooks. 'I reckon he'd have had me on the ropes. Good bloke underneath it all.'

'He's OK. Andy, why are you down here without Griff? It can't be safe. There's room for him here—'

'I'd rather he kept an eye on Ruth.'

'One of his henchmen, then.'

'Oh, the police are so keen to make something stick, I can't wipe my arse without them knowing,' he said, so airily I could have strangled him. He strolled over to the front window, pulling back the curtains to look out.

'Get away from there, for Christ's sake!' I pulled him away and drew the curtains tightly.

'I was only looking—'

'You don't, when someone's after you, "only do" anything,' I said, furious with my voice for cracking.

'Poor old thing,' he said, stroking my hair as if I were a particularly bedraggled stray cat. 'I'll make you a cup of tea, shall I?'

'What you ought to be doing is looking at Ollie's list. See if there's anyone you've ever beaten at chess.'

'Yes, miss. Sorry, miss.' He took the list from me, and his eyes ranged over it, but he put it down without comment. He went over to the phone. From the number of digits it was long distance. And although he didn't say her name, it was clear he was speaking to Ruth.

I gathered up the mugs and plates. Might as well wash up.

I was drying the last teaspoon when he breezed in. 'They're moving her,' he said. 'Now. To another safe house. Another friend of Griff's. Why don't you leave that to me and go to bed?'

Chapter Nineteen

There was no doubt about it: someone was committing fraud. And it seemed as if it might be on quite a large scale. Gurjit moved the cursor inexorably down the screen, scrolling on to other, equally damning pages.

I had gone to the airport on the earliest evening I could, Monday – to satisfy either her or my conscience, I wasn't sure which – and was now peering at her computer.

'Any idea where it's all going?' I asked.

'I haven't had time even to contemplate that. My job, after all, is a clerical one. I have to complete the requisite amount of work each evening I come here. Goodness knows I've more than enough! Look at that pile – that's the backlog I've got to deal with. Mark said to send them all out together. And when I go home there are my college assignments. I dare not get behind in those. Mr Jagger thought I might obtain As if I continued to work well.'

'Good for you! Look, can you print some of this material off while you continue with your routine work? Then I could have another look without disturbing you.' What I wanted to do was see if a regular pattern emerged: then Gurjit could present her findings to Mark with appropriate recommendations.

She hesitated, then switched on the printer. It purred into life, and a stream of paper emerged, gentle as a caress. I thought about our dot matrix at work. I unwrapped a sandwich. A fire-alarm – false, it transpired – had cut short my lunch, and though I'd promised myself another meal at the Italian place, Richard had called a tea-time meeting about our retention rates. Under the new funding rules the college had to recruit eight per cent more students than the previous year, keep the students whatever their behaviour or aptitude, and make sure it maintained its traditional good exam results. It didn't take a genius to realise that these goals were mutually incompatible, so it was a resentful and frustrated group of people who gathered in an empty classroom. I'd started to chomp surreptitiously on plain biscuits in an attempt to appease my stomach, but had so clearly irritated Richard that I tucked most of the packet into my bag. At least I now had a second course.

Except that Gurjit pointed silently, and, I'd like to think, apologetically, to a notice: NO FOOD OR DRINK IN THIS AREA.

'Tough,' I said. And carried on eating, only to endure the embarrassing spectacle of one of my students crawling round on hands and knees after me gathering up my non-existent crumbs. Perhaps I'd better save the biscuits till later.

Right. The stolen goods.

Asthma sprays.

Generic antibiotics.

Painkillers – aspirin and paracetamol-based.

A variety of preparations I hadn't a clue about: vaccines, by the look of it. Never large quantities, but Swiss and German drugs don't come cheap, so even a small cardboard box might represent several thousand pounds.

I rubbed my hands across my face. The room was too hot and airless; Gurjit's relentless tapping would send me to sleep if I wasn't careful.

'Is this the lot?' I asked, opening my marking bag – a Tesco's carrier, this week.

She jumped. 'Yes. Sophie, you're not taking them away with you, are you?'

'It's nine-thirty, Gurjit, and I've got to be at college at eight tomorrow for the field trip. I'll look at everything as soon as I can. Or you can tell Mark. Or you can call the police. Either would make sense.' And would spare me hours of work.

She looked at me, suddenly very young. 'I'd like everything to make sense before I tell Mark.'

'I still think you should tell him straight away.'

She shook her head.

'And you won't tell the police in case it implicates – someone you don't want implicated.'

'Maybe it will implicate *me*, Sophie.'

'Of course it won't!'

'The relevant dates . . .'

'No! You can see for yourself it's been going on for months. You proved it to me, Gurjit! Come on, all you're doing is exposing it!'

'Whistle-blowers are not always popular.'

'Popular be hanged. Gurjit, please report this.'

She shook her head again.

'Well, why not discuss it with your parents?'

No. Because their advice would be the same as mine, presumably.

'OK. Have I got the lot? Because I'm off now. Are you coming?'

She blushed.

'Or do you have to sign off with someone?'

I barely made out the name Mark. So I smiled, wished her well, and was on my way.

Andy was playing Chopin on my piano when I got back.

'Like that Wilde character,' he said, 'not accurately but with a great deal of feeling. Here, I got you this. The pharmacist said it was more effective in liquid form.'

As presents go, I suppose most people wouldn't rate too highly a bottle of antacid medicine, but I accepted in the spirit it was meant.

'You look done in,' he said. 'Tell me.'

I put my feet on the sofa, and did just that. From no lifts in the morning, to no lunch and no tea, to Gurjit gathering crumbs and the airport fraud. He looked as pale and drawn as I felt at the end of it.

He disappeared into the kitchen, returning with two glasses with ice and lemon. 'G and T. People I know with ulcers seem to get away with that.'

'I haven't got an ulcer!'

'You soon will have, the way you're going on. This is a crazy life, Sophie.'

'No worse than anyone else's.'

'A lot worse than mine. Tell you what – why don't you take a sickie? We could nip off to Wales for a couple of days.'

God, it was tempting.

'I'll get Griff to bring Ruth down too.'

'I don't need a sickie. Nice easy day tomorrow – sheepdog to an Environmental Studies field trip.'

'Where?'

'Bewdley. Look.' I fished out an OS map and pointed out the track we were to follow.

'Nice forecast for tomorrow. Bright and crisp. Tell you what, why don't I come too? I could buy a kagoul in Harborne. My spare wellies are in that cupboard in the garage, – at least, they were. And I wouldn't get hassled by your students – they'd never expect to meet me in a kagoul.'

'Why not? I'll go in to work by bus, and travel to Bewdley on the minibus, as planned – you get your gear and drive my car out to meet me.'

'Right!'

'To be honest, you could save me a lot of embarrassment. The other member of staff is this guy with a thing about me. Carl.'

'Didn't you have a bit of a thing about him?'

'That was then.'

And then we remembered: simultaneously. 'The fuzz.'

'I've got to be at Rose Road by nine,' he continued. 'More of the same. Glad I'm on the right side of the law.'

'You are *now*! I mean, on Saturday they were ready to put you on the rack, weren't they?' I waited but he didn't reply. What had I said? 'I'll turn in now, Andy. Thanks again for this.' There was no way I would be separated from that antacid.

As it was, it took longer than I liked for it to work enough to let me sleep. From downstairs came the sound of Andy's voice on the phone: the call seemed to go on for ages. Perhaps he was phoning Ruth again. Then he went into the kitchen. Presumably he was swilling the glasses – I'd never touched that gin. And then I heard him switching off lights, checking the lock on the front door, coming up to bed.

Then I was awake, and looking out of the window. Something had activated the security light. A fox? And then I heard footsteps, starting up the path.

When I stopped panicking I realised that the car parked across the road was a Panda, and that the figure was a uniformed policewoman. We were being looked after.

Not, it occurred to me, very carefully. What had changed? Why hadn't Chris pressed me to have someone living in? Why did no one insist on driving me everywhere? Once upon a time Chris wouldn't have let me step outside the front door without an escort under these circumstances – had that merely been because he fancied me back then, and now things were cooling I could go hang? But Andy was in the public eye. He was famous. Surely they couldn't afford to let anything happen to him! Damn it, he hadn't even got Griff to call on any more.

My stomach was thoroughly irritable by now, and I was so far from sleep I thought I'd have to clean the entire kitchen to get the pattern back. And then I thought of those homeopathic tablets Griff had given me.

I don't know whether it was the tea-towel drawer, the biscuits or the tablets. Whatever it was, I managed to sleep at last.

This must be a day for miracles. Tuesday broke fine and dry, if very cold, the minibus stood in its allotted place in the windswept car park, and all the students were on time. All except one: Pritpal. Since he was a bit of a poet as well as an environmental scientist, perhaps this was to be expected. He was no doubt knocking off an ode after breakfast. Since we'd actually planned all along to set off at eight-forty-five, we'd only told the students to come at eight-fifteen to urge them on a little – there was plenty of slack.

Carl and I loaded the bags into the minibus, which we were both trained to drive. Then we let the kids aboard. Most had made an effort to wear warm clothes, the girls crushing anoraks over their delicate *kameez* and *salwar*, but their footwear made Carl tear his hair – a mistake, since it was beginning to thin, badly.

'How crazy can you get? I *told* them sensible shoes. Look at those girls – little slip-ons – no protection at all! And that lad – *sandals*, for God's sake!'

I was afraid his voice would carry.

'It's not crazy – it's *poor*, Carl. Even trainers cost. And most of these kids have parents on the dole – or doing badly-paid piece-work in factories. Remember, two-thirds of them are coming free today because they couldn't afford the £3 for the bus. And I suspect their lunchboxes will be revelations.'

'They should get their priorities right.' Carl's glance swept self-righteously over the Gortex and walking boots we both carried.

'On an income like theirs, they probably have. Ah! Prit! How's the sonnet?'

'Sorry I'm late, Sophie. Only it's my dad – he was bad and we had to call in the doctor.' And Prit would have had to translate.

'His gall-bladder again?'

'Won't stick to his diet. Or me mum won't let him.'

'How much sleep did you get?'

'Might have a kip in the coach.'

'Good idea. It's OK,' I overrode Carl, 'we're only just ready.' I ignored Carl's open mouth. 'In you get.' I swung into the driver's seat. 'Make sure you fasten your seat-belts. Right? Off we go!'

Where the sun had not yet penetrated, the verges were white with frost; skid marks in interesting places suggested that other drivers had had more faith in road grit than I did. In any case, the minibus was no rally car, and there were all those precious lives in the back. At least I didn't have to worry about Andy going hell for leather in a car he didn't know in order to meet up with us; and like it or not, he was probably safer in Rose Road nick than anywhere else.

All I had to worry about, then, was the icy road and

Carl's emotions. While I was apparently chaperoning the girls, they were also chaperoning me: perhaps his wife realised that. I hoped so. I'd never seen her lose her temper, but it had always seemed to me that she was on the verge of doing so; part of my attraction for Carl was that I had shoulders broad enough to bear all his troubles, blow-by-blow accounts of their rows included. Now I was no longer in love with him, it did occur to me that perhaps he wasn't blameless, but my own conscience preferred to believe him at least more sinned against than sinning.

I enjoyed the Bewdley bypass, which was dry and encouraging, and then picked my way through narrow lanes until Carl stopped me: this was the lay-by where we were to park, and that the lane we were to follow. The sun was now warm, but the lane was frosty where it wasn't muddy: I laced myself into my boots, and considered all those cheap city shoes with cold feet within. Chilblains, that's what they'd get. Some of them didn't have gloves; I could hardly suggest they held hands inside each other's pockets.

They all had tasks to fulfil, and notes to make. The assignment was on the recreational uses of the river: later in the year they'd go and look at the Severn at Ironbridge Gorge. I appointed myself photographer, because I wanted to keep my distance from Carl; I helped with the odd spelling, but in general maintained a semi-detached relationship with both him and the students. So long as my feet kept steady, my mind was free to wander. We soon turned on to a path through the meadows on the west bank, the river's edge pitted with little hollows which would be occupied on warm Saturdays by Brummie anglers: another recreational use to add to the Severn Valley Railway already on their list.

While they wrote, I listened to the swirl and gloop of the river. It was all remarkably peaceful, and when one of the likelier lads attempted to improve nature with an over-loud dose of his Walkman, I frowned him down. It wasn't just selfishness: goodness knows what such a volume directed straight into his ears would do for his future hearing.

I pointed across the river to some very choice residences. 'I could manage one of those.'

'I'd rather have a secluded cottage in the woods,' Carl replied, his voice just missing an embarrassing intimacy.

'They must be pretty damp if they're round here,' Pritpal said. 'Look at the far bank – you can see how high the water must go. Right up to their foundations.'

Carl beckoned everyone round him for a general discussion on floodplains, and I mooched along on my own for a bit. It was too cold to stand still for long, even if you were as warmly wrapped-up as I was, and the frost crunched under my feet under the trees. I took time to gaze around me – not something I managed to do very often – and breathed a cleaner air than the stuff surrounding William Murdock. The frost had thickened the branches, and they glistened against a deep blue sky. Idyllic. What about a job out here? There were further education colleges in other places than Birmingham, and apart from the choir I had no particular ties. Not any more, it seemed. Yes, I might start looking.

Eventually the others caught up with me, Carl contriving somehow to fall into step with me on a path barely wide enough for two. I could think of nothing to say: nothing at all. At last, biting back a yawn, and for want of anything better, I started to tell him about my work experience activities.

'There's a scheme – though I don't know whether it would apply to us, now William Murdock's no longer under Birmingham Education Committee's umbrella – for staff to get work experience,' he said. 'I was wondering about applying.'

'What sort of experience?'

'Something that'll clear the teacher's head, and also benefit the employer. I could simply do a stint in a pharmacy, I suppose, see if I liked it.'

There was a pregnant pause. I was supposed to fill it with an enquiry about how long he'd be gone.

'D'you think they might find something for me?' Damn it, I sounded wistful. 'English teachers might not be as marketable as pharmacists.'

His face suggested he agreed.

Another silence.

'Are those the woods with the cottages?' asked Prit, bounding up beside us. He galloped off to have a look without waiting for an answer.

'Nice kid,' said Carl.

'Hmm. Can't be easy, being a Sikh amidst all these Muslims,' I said. 'Oh, shit! You know what this is, don't you? It's Ramadan! The poor little beggars won't be able to have any lunch. Not even a hot drink when we get back to the minibus.'

'So long as they don't expect us to fast with them,' Carl muttered.

I bit my lip: how could anyone possibly eat in front of people who'd not eaten or drunk since daybreak? And shouldn't we have made some arrangement for them to pray?

At least it wasn't me who'd goofed, but I should have thought of it.

Pritpal came bounding back, gesticulating. 'Come on – it's like Sleeping Beauty or something.'

His face was so full of delight we all speeded up, even the most unsuitably-shod girl.

'There!' He gestured as if he'd stage-managed the whole thing.

A row of four cottages, two pairs of semis. Derelict.

'OK,' said Carl, going into teacher mode but destroying the spell, 'all of you, work out everything you can. Age – when they were abandoned – everything.'

Work out the little comedies and tragedies of unknown, long-gone people: just like that. I wandered up to the gates, securely fastened with padlocks and chains. Actually at close quarters they weren't so romantic. They even had garages, opening on to the track on which we now stood. You could still just about distinguish once-spruce lawns; though which were flower and which vegetable beds no one could possibly tell. A Fairy Liquid bottle stood on a front door step; dead clematis spidered down a tottering trellis.

'Are you all right?'

I'd forgotten about Carl.

'Ordinary people and their ordinary lives – and it all comes to this.'

'Like Prit said, it's very damp. Trees on three sides, the

river to the front . . . Inconvenient, too. No buses. You'd have to walk or drive all the way we've come, plus some more, to get into the town centre.'

'Not much work either,' I added, in teacher mode myself. 'Forestry or agriculture for the men, service for the women. I suppose you'd grow most of what you needed to eat.' In my mind's eye I saw neat rows of beans, lettuces, cabbages.

'You wouldn't want to eat that, though,' Carl said, pointing to a plant managing to flower despite the cold. 'Wasn't it you who wanted to know about helleborin? There you are: winter hellebore.'

'You're joking!'

'Common enough garden plant. Look, there's some parsley over there. And those stalks would be mint.'

'Do wish you'd stop talking about food,' said Halima, a bright girl I was hoping would go on to university. She flicked back her hair, cut shorter than mine, and laughed. 'It's making me dribble.'

'You'll have to spit it out then,' said Mahmood, a youth I hardly knew but whose further acquaintance I might possibly forego. 'In Ramadan you do not swallow even your own saliva. And find something to cover your head.'

'The Holy Koran tells us that purdah is optional.' She stuck her hands deeply into her trouser pockets. 'And let me tell you this, Mahmood, I have read the Koran. For myself.'

'What can a woman understand?' Mahmood responded contemptuously.

Prit caught my eye, and raised his own heavenwards. I tried and failed to ignore his appeal, but responded more sensibly by remembering I was supposed to be group photographer. I shot off half a dozen more frames, and the expedition moved on.

The house was properly locked when I got back, and the living-room curtains drawn. So Andy had been back, but was now out again. A new Andy, considerate enough to leave a large note where I couldn't miss it:

PLAYING CHESS WITH ONE OF THE ROSE ROAD LADS. C U LATER.

In the kitchen there was an aromatic casserole and a plate covered with clingfilm. My supper, courtesy Mr Rivers. Pasta. There was also a half-bottle of a soft red Rioja with a note from Ian:

I RECKON RED'S KINDER ON THE STOMACH THEN WHITE. TRY IT! ID.

And it was.

Chapter Twenty

I'd just parked and was waiting in the foyer for one for the two lifts supposedly in operation when Richard appeared at my shoulder.

'How did the trip go yesterday?' The tone of his voice suggested he expected at least one death and two cases of beri beri.

'Bewdley? Fine! All the kids turned up, the minibus behaved itself, Carl pronounced himself happy with all the work done and I took photographs of everything in sight.'

He perked up. 'Photos? I want to do a display board for Parents' Evening so perhaps . . .'

'But that's tomorrow!'

'You haven't got the films on you?'

'I thought I might slip out to Five Ways at lunchtime and drop them into Boots.'

'But there's the Board of Study meeting at twelve!'

'And I'm teaching till five-thirty. So it doesn't look as if you'll have any photos, Richard. Sorry.'

'You couldn't nip off now, I suppose? Leave your bag – I'll take that up.' He eyed it with resignation: you didn't associate Tesco's carriers with Heads of Division. 'You should be back by nine, but if you're not I'll let your students in.'

'Thanks, Richard.' Thanks a lot.

I suppose there was some weather between nine and four, but if there was I didn't notice it. Whoever designed William

Murdock – and those of us who knew and loved the place would condemn the looseness of my verb – made the windows so high you couldn't see out if you were sitting down, and of course, there were no windows in the corridors or stairwells which formed the inner core of the building. Since Wednesday turned out to be a sitting-down day, and the lights had been on most of the time, the first I knew about the weather being anything other than plain cold and windy was a rush of students to the windows at about three-forty. Snow! Horizontal across the window. I have this fantasy that one day the entire student population will run to the windows and the whole building will collapse outwards, as if a giant banana were being unpeeled: but today was marked by no more than the usual chorus of demands from the students that they be sent home immediately, before the buses stopped running. Unfortunately in these days of charters, they are guaranteed a full working day whether they want one or not, and it would have taken someone with a good deal more temerity than I could muster to let them go. Whispered staff colloquies in corners between classes certainly involved prayers that evening classes be cancelled, but Management had given no such order when I left, feeling a total rat, at five-thirty. True, there weren't many managers around; Richard's was the only important car still in the car park.

The worst part of the weather wasn't the snow, but the wind which whipped into a frenzy, at the same time making a mockery of my short skirt and thick tights. Mini-kilts might be fun and flirty, but they guaranteed a cold bum.

I sat in the traffic jam – warm enough now, thanks to the Renault's heating – and fantasised about the evening. Warmth figured largely in that, too.

For some reason my central-heating never coped with a north-easterly wind: this would certainly defeat it, just as it was defeating the salt and grit on the roads. Already the three lanes of the Five Ways Island were reduced to two. A childish prayer that tomorrow the roads might be impenetrable and that college would be closed passed my lips. A whole day off!

But tonight, I had to cook – possibly for two – and sort

out the wretched airport papers for Gurjit. I'd better pop into Safeway, just in case.

In case of siege? Everyone else had had the same idea, and the place was as crowded as if they were giving the stuff away. There wasn't a single candle left on the shelves: what was everyone expecting?

Andy was home and busy in the kitchen, scrubbing potatoes. A couple of portions of Christmas-holiday cooked casserole were defrosting on the hob.

'Here,' he said, passing me a glass of Valdepenas. 'No, on second thoughts, wait until you've eaten. Got to look after that stomach. Anything else need doing?'

'You wouldn't fancy a real fire, would you?' How stupid! A fire might be a treat for me, but he regularly had huge, baronial, open-hearthed affairs down in Devon.

'Brilliant,' he said. 'Is there still some of Uncle Bert's smokeless fuel in the shed? I'll go and get a couple of buckets.'

And then it was time to start on those papers. I finished the table-clearing Andy and Chris had started on Sunday, and laid everything out, together with a pencil and pad; Andy merely raised an eyebrow, and took himself off the far end of the table. He produced files of his own, and a pad. But his pencil was gold.

An hour's work showed me that while consignments of medicine came in from Germany and Switzerland on several nights of the week, the only night they went adrift was Wednesday. There were two conclusions possible: either someone who worked only on Wednesday night was stealing them; or they could only be disposed of on a Wednesday night or, presumably, early on Thursday. So I needed two things: the staff roster and a schedule of outgoing lorries. And planes, on reflection. It was beyond me. This was a job for professionals with time and resources. Dave Clarke, Fraud Squad: he'd walk all over it. His numbers – work and home – were in my diary, in my handbag, beside me—

But I'd promised Gurjit I'd do nothing.

'What's the matter? You look – fraught.' Andy looked at

me, all concern. He pushed his papers away and leaned forward, elbows on the table. 'Tell your Uncle Andy.'

'I wish I could. It's confidential.'

'You know me: silent as the grave.'

It was so tempting: A confidant, ready to give advice . . .

'I've got a student on work experience who thinks someone's defrauding her employer. She's got these print-outs for me. I *think* they prove she's right.'

'So go to the police.'

'She's sworn me to secrecy. She's afraid of two quite separate things: either she's wrong and she could look a fool in front of her boss, or it's her boss who's doing it.'

'Evidence?'

I shook my head. 'I would say it wasn't her boss. He wouldn't steal on Wednesday nights only, would he?'

'What?'

'The stuff only goes missing on Wednesday night. No other night, just every Wednesday! Someone's probably nicking a box even as we speak.'

'And you can work that out just from those print-outs?'

What on earth was that in his voice? Not amusement or disbelief: I looked up sharply. No matter how he might try to disguise it, his face was troubled. But it couldn't be. It didn't make sense.

'So what do you propose to do now?'

'Nothing, till the morning. I don't have the student's number, and I shouldn't think she's made it to the airport tonight, not in this weather.'

'Airport? What, Birmingham International? Surely not! Security there must be absolutely watertight!'

'West Midlands Airport. Out towards Lichfield. It's mostly freight, including medical supplies – which are getting diverted. On Wednesday nights.'

'Any idea why?'

'I'd guess there's a bent parcels carrier on that night.'

'Of course! So you'll—'

'Andy, I don't want to get involved. It's nothing to do with me! None of my business!' I got up dramatically; and sat down sharply as that bloody spear pierced my stomach.

I got up more slowly and found the stomach medicine in the kitchen.

'See?' I said, coming back into the living room. 'Even my stomach wants me to leave it alone.'

'I should say your stomach's quite right.' He got up and came to my end of the table.

'Hey, what are you doing? No, Andy, they're all in order!'

He was scooping them roughly together. 'Burn them. Get rid of the evidence. End of problem.'

'No. It wouldn't be.'

'You could tell the student she was wrong. She'd be happier.'

'She wouldn't believe me! She knows what's wrong. If I don't help, she'll talk to her boss – eventually.'

'What'll you do with the papers?'

I smiled. 'That's easy. I've got a little floor safe. After my house was done over, I thought I'd better treat myself.'

'And then?'

'Start talking to the Fraud Squad. You wouldn't like to come along with me, would you?'

'What the fuck—'

'Just to protect me,' I said as lightly as I could; it must be twenty years since I'd last seen Andy so angry. And I had no idea why. 'There's this inspector who can't wait to get his hands in my knickers. Is that the time? I'd really like to watch the weather forecast.'

Enough snow had fallen by bed-time to suggest I would indeed be cut off from college tomorrow. The silence was disconcerting: Harborne, if not the whole of Birmingham, had closed down. I decided to leave the central-heating on low all night, and prepared to sleep. Except, of course, my brain settled down to have a good worry about Andy, who had been off-hand or abstracted, depending on the amount of charity I could muster, for the rest of the evening. At about one, my stomach decided to join in, so I went downstairs – to clean out the spice rack, this time – and to have an illicit milky drink and biscuits.

Hell! It was too cold for the spice rack. Just the drink

and the biscuits then. Look after the stomach and let the sleep patterns look after themselves.

It was warmer in the living room than in the kitchen, so I took my drinking chocolate and biscuits through and plonked myself down on the sofa. That spear again: it wanted me to eat sitting upright. OK, the dining table and a straight-backed chair, if that was the way it wanted it. I'd tidied my papers away into the safe I'd had fitted in my upstairs loo, but Andy's lay scattered where he had left them. Headed paper – his Foundation, no doubt. Reports; accounts; projections – really exciting stuff. I found it hard to reconcile Andy the irresponsible idiot with Andy the concerned Director. Looking at them more closely, I was amazed at how much money his Foundation was raising – but then, the outgoings were enormous. Andy subscribed to the theory that if you paid peanuts you got monkeys, and he wanted to maintain attractive employment on the African subcontinent for men and women who'd been born there. I'd seen a TV programme about Sierra Leone which showed the plight of doctors and nurses who hadn't been paid in months, whose only chance of survival was emigration. The Foundation was trying to find ways of funding them without allowing governments to abrogate their responsibilities. There were consultation papers from Oxfam, ActionAid and Christian Aid: Andy was clearly a man to be reckoned with.

At the bottom of the pile was an internal memo from his hospital accountant. Problems with auditors . . .?

These were confidential papers. *Andy's.* I had no right to be reading them. Hurriedly, I rearranged them to a rough approximation of their previous positions, and returned to the kitchen for more stomach medicine. Bed, that was where I ought to be. Even if the roads were impassable by car, there were always buses – not to mention legs. And that meant getting up earlier.

But what if the college itself was closed? I said a silent prayer and reset the radio-alarm to Radio WM, so I'd hear the good news from the comfort of my duvet.

Chapter Twenty-One

The college was open: at least, it wasn't on Radio WM's closed list. So I'd better struggle in. I left the car under its personal snow-drift and headed for the bus. The roads were amazingly free of both snow and traffic, and the bus sped through, dropping me at Five Ways ten minutes earlier than usual. This might have been a mixed blessing, had I not seen a woman opening up the shop where I'd left my films. So I could give Richard what he wanted, and be in college on time: not that any of the students had similar impulses.

I stopped off at the eighth floor to let Richard choose his photographs and also to see how he was. He was just emerging from the lift as I staggered from the stairwell.

'Just think,' I said, watching him put down his briefcase and unlock his office door, 'this time next year you'll be able to lie in bed and not worry about the weather!'

'Hmm,' he said absently. Then, 'Sorry – I could have given you a lift, couldn't I?'

'No problem – I used the trusty bus. But I'd be very grateful for a lift tonight after Parents' Evening – if we're still running it, that is.' I looked out at the snow, in stylised Christmas-card drifts against the window.

He sighed. 'Makes sense to cancel, doesn't it? But how do we contact the parents?'

'I don't think there were all that many coming anyway,' I said, hopefully.

'There are always those who come in on spec.'

'Half the colleges in Brum are closed for the day. Most people seem to have assumed that we are, too.'

‘The place is like the *Marie Celeste*, isn’t it? I’ll talk to the principal, see what he thinks.’

‘Maybe you should talk to those of us who are actually involved? Malcolm – he’s in charge of the A-level course, he might have an opinion.’

‘But Worrall could over-rule him anyway. *Would* over-rule him, in his present state of mind.’ He looked glum.

I pointed to the calendar. ‘How many more days?’

But even that didn’t cheer him up.

The whole day had been a waste of time, with a full complement of staff but the barest smattering of students. We’d all taught as best we could, but there was a dilemma: did you teach new material to the two or three in front of you who were entitled to it, or save it for a full house another day?

I spent the latter part of the afternoon helping Malcolm stick name and subject signs on classroom doors so parents would know where to find us, had a Kit-kat and a cup of tea, and installed myself in the room set aside for English teachers. Malcolm’s chart showed me I could expect Mr and Mrs Aftab at five, Mrs Phipps at six-thirty and Mr Bansal at eight. Not very promising, so I took along my marking, not as much as usual since I’d only got this week’s. The backlog had been dealt with by other hands than mine; I tried not to remember the wreath, and the mess inside my car, of course. Five-thirty, and a breathless Florence brought me a phone message from the Aftabs: she’d fallen on the ice as she set out and broken her wrist. OK. I’d prepare a couple more stories from *Dubliners.* By seven it was apparent that Mrs Phipps too would not be coming.

The other English teachers were deep in their own marking and preparation, with only about six sets of parents between them so far. I tried the usual displacement activities. I examined the notices and posters on the wall: there was some nice project work on the Third World which Andy would have approved, and more on the environment. Out of the curtainless windows it was cold and dark, though not snowing; buses ran with their usual frequency. Some youths were snowballing hapless motorists. And my stomach was beginning to demand something more substantial than antacids.

Trying to ignore it, I found some scrap paper in my bag, and tried to focus on the subject of the airport thefts. It was the Wednesday business that fascinated me. Why just that night?

I didn't have long to think about it, however. A tap at the door announced Mr and Mrs Bansal. He was smoothly affluent in a double-breasted suit and vicuna coat slung across his shoulders; she – much more delicate-featured than Gurjit – wore a well-cut camel coat over a sari and endearing sheepskin boots.

'I do hope we're not disturbing you. Only I thought – with the poor weather – and if you had no one else with you—'

'Nonsense! You can see she's on her own, my love. A really bad show, this, Miss Rivers. No one making the effort. I thought we could have a really good chinwag about our little girl.'

I smiled at them equally and gestured them to chairs.

'I'm worried about this airport business,' he said, tweaking his trousers and shooting his cuffs as he settled down; I noticed his watch was a Rolex. 'The amount of time it takes from her studies! And yet she tells me you recommended it.'

'She's only in her first year—'

'No, my love, I want to hear what Miss Rivers has to say.'

'I agree with your wife,' I said, remembering too late the importance of tact in these matters. 'It is only her first year, and it's valuable practical experience for her. It will look excellent on her UCAS form when she applies to university, and it'll be useful for her Record of Achievement, too.'

'But her work – however good her application, it's the results that butter parsnips.'

'As far as I know, she's keeping up with her work. Remember, I don't actually teach her. What do her lecturers and her tutor say?'

'They seem very pleased—' Mrs Bansal began.

'Of course they are! She's a good girl. But is she good enough? I'm not talking about just any university, I want her to go to a good one. International Law at Exeter. I rather fancied that.'

'It's a very good course at a very good university,' I agreed. 'Is that what she wants to do?'

'I rather thought she—'

'You know what these girls are – come now, you're only a girl yourself, Miss Rivers! – they can't make up their minds. All of a sudden she doesn't know if she wants to leave Birmingham. I tell her, many families we know won't *let* their daughters leave Birmingham. You need to stretch your wings and fly, I tell her.'

I had a terrible feeling that that was exactly what she might want to do. Perhaps I should try an oblique approach. 'She's very lucky having such enlightened parents. So many of our students are being whisked away into arranged marriages.'

'Ah! Muslims! What else would you expect?'

'Ours was an arranged marriage,' she said.

'Yes, but that was years ago. Move with the times, that's what I always say. Plenty of time when she's qualified, anyway.' He rubbed his hands in delight.

For all his bonhomie, I thought now was not the time to ask how he felt about mixed-race marriages.

'I tell her, if she gets three As, I'll buy her a Merc. A lady's car – that convertible. Then we'll think about a nice boy. A barrister, a consultant – that sort of thing.'

Not a training officer at a middle-sized airport. Of Caucasian origin.

'Tell you what,' I said, 'I'll talk to the airport people and make sure they don't ask her to work too many hours. She's so willing it would be terribly easy for them to take advantage of her.'

'She'd have been there tonight but we were worried about the snow,' she said. And then she flashed a most knowing and amused smile. 'I think she enjoys the company.'

'Oh, yes, a very fine company. I used to know their man in Nairobi. Very fine. Played an excellent round of golf. Do you know him, Miss Rivers – a Mr Cartwright? Ex-RAF.'

I shook my head. 'I've only met the training officer.' And added mentally, ex-Fire.

Richard insisted on running me home. It wasn't far out of his way, but he looked so tired and drawn I felt very guilty.

'Last one of those, thank goodness,' he said, parking behind my Renault. 'I wonder if they do any good? You always get the parents you don't need to see – never those with problem kids. And there's the whole problem of parental involvement anyway, when students are over eighteen. Not to mention the fact that most of our parents aren't English speakers.'

'Get interpreters. Or better still, ask the students along too. Make it a review evening.'

'Talk to Malcolm about it. None of my business. Not any more.'

'But you'll be coming back here to do a little part-time teaching? Everyone knows you're a brilliant teacher. Everyone assumed you'd do some A-level work next September—'

'No. I won't be coming back.' His voice mixed anger and pain.

'What?'

'Not allowed to.'

'What!'

'Not allowed to. There was a note in my in-tray this morning. Funding arrangements. When you retire you can go and teach somewhere else, but not the place you've left.' He sounded ineffably bitter.

'So after thirty-odd years—'

'I'm on the scrap-heap. I suppose it makes sense – either you're fit to do your job or you're not. But teaching four or five hours a week isn't the same as doing what I'm doing now. Twelve hours a day, and every weekend, running just to stand still. I'd have enjoyed teaching again. Not that the place is what it used to be. All these people leaving.'

I nodded. People moved on – my old friend Philomena had escaped back into nursing – but he was right. When new people came, there wasn't the time to spend getting to know them; very few of us seemed to find the time or energy to socialise after work.

We sighed in unison, and I glanced at his profile.

'Fancy a drink?' I asked on impulse. Goodness knew how he and Andy would get on.

'Love one.' As he locked up, he added, 'Home's not very welcoming—' He dropped his voice, and I didn't hear the rest.

At first I pretended not to have heard at all. Halfway up the drive, however, I stopped. 'Are there – problems?'

'Sheila's left me.' Just like that. In the cold night, on my drive. His voice was almost inaudible again. 'For another woman. I've been too embarrassed—'

'Oh, Richard.' You couldn't cuddle your boss. So I touched his arm, and almost scooped him into the house.

While we talked, Andy made sandwiches and plied our unexpected guest with Laphroaig. I ate; Richard drank.

In the end I drove his car home, while Andy followed in mine. Richard wasn't that drunk, just tired; tired of being married to William Murdock, tired of having a perfect wife so bored by William Murdock widowhood she'd taken up painting. At art college she'd discovered her artistic potential – and her sexuality, with a woman lecturer. And Richard had so been looking forward to retirement.

Between us we got him up to bed, took off his shoes and suit and shoved him under the duvet.

'Poor bastard,' Andy said.

And there was very little I could add to that.

Chapter Twenty-Two

Was it was really only ten-thirty when we got home? We staggered into the living room, where Andy polished off the sandwiches I'd had my eye on, and then, chastened, made some more, thus reducing my bread reserves to nil. Friday breakfast would have to be white sliced from the newsagent, provided one of us was noble enough to go and get it. Then I remembered some rolled oats at the back of a cupboard, and put them to soak for old-fashioned and warming porridge.

'Want to look at the photos of our trip?' I asked casually, dredging them out of my bag before they got forgotten and squashed, the usual fate of the sediment therein. I put them on the dining table: Andy's papers were there, and when I leant over them to pick up Richard's whisky glass, I could feel his eyes on me. Still holding the glass, I turned to him.

'This discrepancy the auditor mustn't find,' I said, 'wouldn't have anything illegal behind it, would it?'

'For Christ's sake—'

'Because something stinks, Andy. Something stinks about your behaviour, since the day I came upon you at Five Ways right up to now.' I found myself getting more and more in the mood for confrontation. 'You're up to something. And if you're up to what I think you're doing, that stinks too.'

He turned away from me.

'What is it? Drugs?' There was a tiny jerk of his shoulders. 'The squeaky-clean Andy screwing up his life again?'

'You know me better than that!' He wheeled round to face me.

'That's just where you're wrong. I *don't* know you, not like you are now. What are you up to?'

'Nothing.' His face was unreadable: anger, frustration and something else. Fear?

'OK, so what are your associates up to? I don't buy that story of you coming to Brum to check out the Music Centre – you've never been that conscientious. And I saw you the other day, when you were supposed to be safely tucked up in the north – what were you doing?'

'What's it to do with you?'

'If you need to ask that – get real, Andy. Crime isn't fun, it's detectable.'

'Who said anything about crime?'

'Is there another explanation?'

'I don't owe you explanations!'

'You owe me the truth!' I slammed the glass on the table. He owed me *everything*, didn't he? Reading, swimming, wobbling along on his first bike – I'd taught him all those. And I'd smuggled food and books to his room when he was supposed to be in disgrace, got together the money for his first girlfriend's abortion. What hadn't I done? And didn't he know it? And where had being kind and supportive and non-judgmental got me?

He clenched his fists and took a step towards me; he grabbed the glass and dashed it at the wall. 'Just bloody shut up!'

Shutting up was the one thing I couldn't do. 'They're losing drugs from the airport. Medicinal drugs. Your hospital is gaining drugs which worry the accountant. You turn up in Birmingham. You are evasive, deceitful. You codpiece for Africa! You'd die for Africa! You'd steal. That's it, isn't it? You'd steal for Africa. Jesus Christ, you're *right* to steal for Africa, I'd do it myself. I'd have helped you, if you'd asked. But the way you did it, you're going to be found out. It *has* been found out. Gurjit'll shop you. Where will your precious Foundation be then? And your job for the United Nations?'

'It's only private hospitals. Never NHS ones. Anyhow, they'll never prove anything.'

'Of course they bloody will! They've got the records of the German and Swiss companies. They've got computerised records saying that planes carrying X-amount of goods have landed. They've got invoices from the airport to the distributors, even if they haven't all been sent out yet because Gurjit is as slow as she's meticulous. Any moment now, someone is going to ask why goods they've been invoiced for haven't arrived. And I'll tell you why they haven't arrived. They've been nicked. You have an accomplice who unloads planes on Wednesday nights and transfers them. I'd bet this year's holiday there's a plane taking off on Wednesday nights to – where? Nairobi? Lagos? Somewhere you can bribe the airport authorities to let a couple of extra boxes through. Somewhere with transport to Mwandara. No. Don't tell me.'

'Of course I shan't fucking tell you! You sleep with a policeman, for Christ's sake!'

'I wouldn't tell Chris—'

'Don't you talk in your sleep any more?'

'Andy, listen to me. I reckon I can sort the computer and the invoices. There's always a chance you'll get away with this – but there's always the chance that Gurjit will tell. Christ, I've been begging her to go to the police!'

He bent to pick up the glass, gathering the shards with his left hand and dropping them into his right.

'Andy – there's something else. Someone else knows, don't they? The person who's trying to kill you?'

'*Kill* someone for doing good? Surely not – ! Oh!' It was a cry of surprise, not pain; he looked at the blood welling up in his palm and held it out to me.

It was easy after that. Straight into big-sister mode, shooing him into the kitchen and grabbing a wodge of kitchen towel.

'What the fuck are you doing? Get some gloves on, woman!' With his left hand he pushed me away.

'What – ?'

'I said, put some gloves on. No holes in your washing up-gloves? Here!'

'Andy – you haven't—'

'Of course I bloody haven't! I had the test before – I mean, I wouldn't put Ruth at risk, would I? But there's all sorts of blood-borne diseases in the camps. I think there's still some glass in there – have you got any tweezers?'

He was downstairs, fully dressed and stirring the porridge, by the time I surfaced. He didn't lift his eyes from the pan: that was the nearest I'd get to an apology. I reached for bowls and spoons.

'No need. I've already laid the table.' He reached out his arm to pull me in for a hug. 'I've been out of order, kid, haven't I? Not just last night, but all along.' He kissed my hair. 'Now, about your offer . . . Can you disguise things a bit? Muddy the waters so – you know, it isn't just me, but it's the guy who helped, and the Foundation, and—'

'I'll do my best.' When and how?

'No risks?'

What the hell did he think I'd be doing, if not taking risks? 'No risks.'

He gave the porridge a final stir. 'Right, that's ready. Breakfast is served, ma'am.'

I was impressed: he'd not only found placemats, he'd also put the Golden Syrup on a plate to catch the dribbles. I looked longingly at it, picked up the brown sugar and a tiny spoon, but finally cast calorific caution to the winds.

While he ate, he inspected the photographs: the river; the kids; the railway viaduct, Carl looking miserable; the cottages. 'Good God. That was where some of Freya's relations used to live.'

'Not really!' I was on my feet, looking over his shoulder.

'See there – they used to have a swing from that tree. There's the rope.'

'Tell me about her relatives,' I said, very quietly putting down my porridge spoon.

'It was her father's side, I think. Cousins . . . No, her mother's. Must have been, because they had a different surname from Freya. Unusual. God knows what it was. Anyway, there was a family of them. The dad was in jail more than he was out of it because he couldn't keep his hands off other people's game – silly sod. The mother, she was a nice little thing, ever so tiny. You'd never have expected her to produce all those children. Five or six. Goodness knows when they were together long enough to beget them, what with his nocturnal activities and his time in jug. Tea?'

'In a minute. Tell me about the children.' I tried to sound casual: the more relaxed he was, the more likely to creep up on long-lost memories.

'Well, there were four girls. One was a bit simple – special needs, I suppose you'd call it these days. That was – God! – Catriona. Then there was Fenella. And Eleanor. She went off for nurse training but hurt her back and had to give up. The youngest was Genevora. Goodness knows where they got all those names from. They weren't really the fanciful type.'

'What about the boys?'

'Simon – they were spared the fancy nomenclature – how's that for a good bit of vocab, oh English teacher?'

'Very impressive. Tell me about Simon.'

'Went into forestry. There weren't all that many jobs round there.'

'And—?'

'Can't remember the name of the other one. He was only a kid. Pretty bright, as I recall. I remember he went to university – pride and joy of the family!'

Under the table I dug my fingers into my palms. *Sound casual!* 'What did he study?'

He shook his head. 'He dropped out anyway, I seem to recall. *Craig!* That was it! But he hated his name – used some nickname.' He ran his spoon one last time round the dish. 'Why all this interest, anyway?'

I pointed to an obscure plant in the corner of one of the photos. 'Because that, Andy, is winter hellebore.'

There was no getting away from it. I had to set out for work, and the chances were I'd be late. All I could do was phone Ian, and equip Andy with that list of roadies he'd so studiously ignored, in the hope that he'd pick out a name – surname, nickname, whatever – that would jog his memory. Then the police could take over. No more nasty hints; no more crimes.

At least we wouldn't be on the receiving end. I'd be at the committing end, wouldn't I? Sooner or later, I had to talk my way into the airport, talk Gurjit out of acting as I'd advised her to act only days before, and undo all her good work. Oh, and not be detected in the doing.

I was just off to my first class when the phone on my desk started ringing. Obeying an imperative I always resented but was powerless to resist, I picked it up.

'Miss Rivers' secretary, if you please.'

Me? A secretary? A photocopy card would be a start.

'This is Sophie Rivers. How can I help?'

'Ah, I didn't expect to reach you so easily, my dear Miss Rivers. Now, we've had a spot of bother here. I've found that Gurjit has got behind in her college studies and I will no longer be letting her work at the airport.'

'Surely, Mr Bansal – all her lecturers said—'

'My word is final. She must get those grades. She missed handing in the last Law assignment, and that put the tin lid on it. I would be grateful if you could notify the appropriate authorities. Good day to you, Miss Rivers.'

'Mr Bansal! Mr Bansal? Shit!'

The bastard! How dare he mess around with the poor kid's life? Didn't she deserve a chance to run it herself? I would have loved to pick up the phone and tell him precisely what I thought of him, but even as I fulminated I realised that I might turn the situation to my – or at least, to Andy's – advantage. But it was still dangerous.

My plan was to go to the first part of the choir's rehearsal as usual, then feign a headache and ostensibly return home. In fact, I'd go to the airport and, using the passwords I remembered, get into the computer system. If anyone challenged me, I now had an excuse: I'd promised Gurjit that I'd tidy things up for her. Yes, I liked that. And tidying was precisely what I'd be doing. So I taught my way efficiently through the day, only breaking off to phone Andy to check on his progress.

'Malpass,' he said, promptly and carelessly. There was no evidence that we had anyone listening in, but I was getting paranoid.

'Don't tell me any more. Get Ian to come and collect you, OK? Don't say anything over the phone.'

I decided to take no chances. I phoned Ian myself. Surely no one'd bother to tap all William Murdock's calls, and surely to goodness a police line wouldn't have eavesdroppers . . .

'There's a name on a list of the roadies who worked on his show that Andy knows. Malpass. And this guy just happens to have lived in a house with winter hellebore growing in the garden. From winter hellebore you get—'

'Helleborin! Well done, Sophie. Right, I'll collect young Andy and see if we can dig up any motive. Any ideas?'

'Well, Andy married this man's cousin, and she subsequently died. But other than that – none.'

'Weird. Well, leave it to me. And remember we've got that wine-tasting tomorrow.'

'*Tomorrow!* Ian, I—'

'Just mind you don't get a cold. OK?'

I'd rarely known Ian so affable. It made my plans for the evening seem even more impossible.

We were trying to convince our music director that we simply couldn't sustain his tempi when someone's mobile phone beeped. The miscreant switched it off, blushing, but then retreated to the loo: he came back dramatically waving his arms.

Naturally our attention switched from the conductor.

'You should see it outside!' he yelled. 'And there's a severe weather warning from the police. They're expecting a foot of snow! They're stopping the buses at nine o'clock.'

It was fortunate we had no important concert the following day: as one person we got to our feet and prepared to leave. Oh, yes – me too. I was desperate to retreat to safety.

But I had that job to do first. Better grit my teeth and get on with it.

Gritting the roads would have been more apposite. The Renault was a sure-footed little car, but it didn't like the side-road I was parked on. It took ages to find a suitable rut for it, and then it was buffeted by the wind so hard I was constantly afraid of losing control. I sat in a mini-jam waiting to get on to the main road and thought.

It was a good job I'd always followed the dictum that there is more than one way of skinning a cat. On my desk at home, I had a modem: I also knew the access password. Right. Home, and hack from there. It was infinitely safer. I could alter the paper records on Monday, going in at a time when the airport staff would be expecting Gurjit and say I'd come to finish off her loose ends. It wouldn't take very long.

A set of tracks led away from my front door. Bad weather for burglars, this. They went straight across to a rectangle of thinner snow in which I parked my car. Or did they? There seemed to be a confusion of prints from the two houses opposite. Odd to be looking at a new house in this weather: the For Sale sign had been up long enough in more clement conditions without exciting any interest. And the people directly opposite me – a couple ten years younger than Aggie but with a tenth of her pzazz – had suddenly started to have a lot of visitors: their family developing pre-Will consciences, perhaps.

Andy had locked the door from the inside – it was unnerving to have him develop common-sense at this stage. So I unlocked both the Chubb and the Yale, and, kicking the snow back off the step, picked my way inside, knowing conclusively as I did so that my waterproof boots were leaking.

'Can I watch you?' Andy asked as I outlined my plans. He was making more soup and promising to do wonderful things with pasta: he must be very penitent indeed. When he revealed the source of a rich fruity smell was pears baking in red wine, it was clear he was seeking absolution, pure and simple.

Which was one thing I couldn't give him. I'd seen hacking done, but had never done it myself; and even if I cleared the relevant bits, a real expert would be able to tell what I'd taken from the hard disk. It all depended how closely they looked.

'Sophie? I said—'

I shook my head. 'Hacking's not a spectator sport. Not the way I do it.' *The way I do it!* As if I made a hobby of it! 'It's going to be slow and very boring, and I may not succeed at all. By the way,' I added, trying to take my mind off the whole affair, 'who was your visitor?'

'Griff.'

'Where the hell's he been all this time? Shouldn't someone have been looking out for you?'

'You've only just got round to asking? Call yourself my minder?'

'I don't. So where's he been?'

'The police relieved him of his duties for a bit. They thought he might interfere with their surveillance. Probably why I've escaped unscathed so far. Chummie must have seen them around, been scared off. Griff came to give me a letter from Ruth.' He patted it where it lay on the table: it was very long.

'How is she?'

'Fine! Voice back to normal. She reckons it was caused by the herb teas she's been drinking – some allergy. I don't see it myself. You can't go wrong with what's organic and natural.'

'You can be allergic to the most innocuous things in nature – dogs and cats, not to mention all those nice country flowers. Hellebore's a flower, come to think of it . . . Andy,' I said, pushing myself from the table, 'I'll eat later. I'm off upstairs now, to my study.'

'You mean that little box room? You usually work down here.'

'I've got the printer and modem up there. Now, I mustn't be interrupted. Tell anyone who should phone I'm flat out with a migraine – OK?'

It was better not to allow him time to reply, so I strode out briskly, ran up the stairs, and closed the door.

I'd expected myself to be sick with apprehension. To fumble hopelessly. I'd even written down the password, lest I forget it at the psychological moment. But I was so calm I frightened myself. And because I was calm, it was easy. Mechanical. If I ever left William Murdock, perhaps I could write a Hackers' Handbook. I erased the offending lines and closed down the system: whoever now tried to print from them would get the same, innocuous invoices. Standing and stretching – perhaps it had generated more tension than I'd realised – it occurred to me that since I knew who the continental suppliers were, I could have a go at rewriting their files too. Retrieving all Gurjit's papers from my little safe, I settled down for a more earnest hack. But my concentration wasn't such that I could ignore the front doorbell followed by a man's voice directly under my feet.

Chris! What the hell was he doing at this hour, and in this weather? There was no time to get the paperwork back into the safe – he'd see me scuttling along the landing – so I shoved it into my marking file. Better get out of the system quickly. Come on, come on . . .

Why the hell wasn't Andy keeping him downstairs? Shit! But the screen was just asking if I'd finished when he burst in.

No, he didn't burst. Not Chris. A more stately entrance you couldn't have imagined. But he'd register the computer screen fading, and the fact that I was using the modem: he couldn't fail to. And there was nervous edge to my voice he'd pick up, for all my striving to be relaxed.

'Not interrupting anything?' he asked.

'Just saving something,' I said, sunny with innocence. And truth. 'But I've finished now.' I stood, and stepped towards him and the door; the room was so narrow he had no option but to back out. 'What brings you here on a night like this?' I asked, trying to sound pleased.

'The night like this. My central-heating's packed up, I've got a bagful of washing and have you eaten? Something smells good.'

Fortunate, really. Or he might have smelt a rat.

I was sure he had, come to think of it. Throughout the meal, he kept looking at me when he thought I wouldn't notice; and afterwards, from the speed Andy checkmated him, his mind couldn't have been on the chessboard. What had he seen? At least I had had a chance to conceal the papers again when I went to the loo. But had Andy said anything to make him suspicious? He was only a musician, not an actor, after all. I was tense and trembling enough to drop the soap powder all over the floor, and I knew I was smiling too much. Andy clearly wanted to catch my eye; I would have loved the chance to reassure him about the hack – not to mention asking what he'd said to Chris, or Chris to him. But, despite getting outside three glasses of Merlot, Chris didn't need the lavatory until we all stood to go to bed.

Then I discovered another thing about breaking the law: it gives you hang-ups about bonking a policeman who trusts you. This time it was I who turned a cold back.

Chapter Twenty-Three

For once the classic inability of a central-heating engineer to predict anything approaching an exact time of arrival was a bonus: it got Chris out of my hair soon after eight. Presumably he had reckoned it would be too cold for him back home to iron his shirts: I could think of no other explanation for their continued presence in my kitchen. Naturally, I ignored them; I had work to do. As I plodded upstairs, however, it struck me that a pile of newly-ironed shirts would offer an exquisite hint of an alibi, a fact which struck Andy less hard than I'd have liked. However, eventually he admitted that ironing had been one of the skills I'd inculcated into him years ago, and he got stuck in, to the accompaniment of Radio Three.

As I fished the papers out of the safe yet again, I had sudden doubts. Was this urge to conceal the material going to betray me? Wouldn't the papers be safer tucked in with my marking? But, rationally, who was going to check up anyway? No one, not if I did my job properly.

Germany turned out to be relatively easy; I emerged stiff but triumphant.

'There! That's that job jobbed,' I said.

'You look knackered. I'll massage your shoulders as soon as you've had your lunch.'

'Lunch?'

'Well, it is nearly two. What'll you have?'

'*Two*!' Relatively easy, was it? When was I going to find time to deal with Switzerland? In the meantime, trying to work out what would be a tasty lunch without any onion or garlic – bearing in mind my evening activities – I headed back upstairs again to hide those papers.

I was too stiff to do any more this afternoon. In fact, despite my leaking boots, making a snowman seemed the ideal occupation. Chris, returning to take Andy and me to the wine-tasting, groped for adequate words to describe our creation – or perhaps he simply found the whole occupation simply beyond his comprehension. At last Andy found a way of making him loosen up. He pelted him with snowballs.

We ought to have won, Ian and I. It was my fault we didn't. I kept on forgetting names of the most familiar grapes.

'Never mind! Third's better than nothing,' said Ian gamely.

'Not when bloody Andy comes in first.' I did not add that having Stephenson come in first with him was even more galling. Presumably it had something to do with the discovery of Malpass's name on that list. And come to think of it, what was she doing sloshing umpteen varieties of wine round her mouth when she and her team should be out locating murder suspects? And, moreover, why, when Chris went to give her a fraternal cheekbuss, did she turn so she took it on the mouth?

I wish I was a better loser.

Sunday started – surprisingly – with a bonk. It continued with breakfast and thence to Chris's for lunch. I predicted, rightly, that he and Andy would lock horns over the chess-board, and had taken my marking and preparation: Joyce, mostly, and *The Dead*. Chris took time off to congratulate me on the excellence of my ironing; I could see the effort it took Andy not to claim the praise for himself. The afternoon drifted into evening, with Chris resolving to stay over till the following morning, and suggesting I made up the spare bed for Andy: obliging of him. And neither Andy nor I could think of a reason not to. Perhaps it was just as well: as bonks went, it was the most adventurous and satisfying I'd ever had with Chris. He even made sure the duvet was tucked round me when he set off at five.

I was up soon afterwards myself, going home to change. I left Andy where he was: apparently Ian had plans which involved collecting him later in the day. So I was alone in my house for a while – long enough to get breakfast, to shower and wash my hair, and go through the post. 'Lonely but free' had been Brahms's motto – I whistled the theme to the *Third Symphony* to remind myself. But the sound echoed round the empty rooms. Maybe I should think of taking in a lodger? Despite the central-heating, I shivered: someone walking over my grave. Not mine, if I could help it! It occurred to me that the little canister Chris had given me might be more useful on my person than in the kitchen: if there were another attack there was no guaranteeing it would be in such a convenient location. I shoved it in my bag.

To work, then. As I parked, Richard drew up: I waited for him, observing the hunch of his shoulders, the down-turned mouth, the greyness of his skin. How long had his hair been silvering? It was white, now, at the temples. All this for a William Murdock that no longer cared about him or the fact that he was wifeless. I found I had opened my arms to cuddle him – a gesture I had quickly to convert to a slapping across the chest against the cold wind. He smiled, if such a wan movement of the mouth can be called a smile, and fell into step beside me. He shot a couple of glances at me, keen, at a guess, to ask me to keep quiet about Thursday night. What could I say? A rhetorical 'Your secret is safe with me?'

'Are you staying on in Brum when you leave?' I asked at last, hoping he'd pick up the sub-text of my question.

He nodded. 'They say you shouldn't do anything in a hurry when you retire.'

'I hope you'll keep in touch,' I said, turning to face him before we went into the foyer. 'You could risk some of my cooking.'

'That's very kind of you,' he began, awkwardly.

I shook my head. 'I should enjoy it. You might not!'

He smiled. Then he nodded his head, almost imperceptibly. Yes: he could trust me not to blab. We waited for the lift together.

As we chugged up, I wondered about Gurjit. It was inevitable that she should seek me out, and I clearly had to say something that would reassure her about her work, both at college and at the airport. What could I say? That I'd like to knee-cap her father? That she should pursue her relationship with Mark, no matter what? Or would she be better to pursue the career her parents – correction, her father – wanted? She was academically gifted, she'd enjoy the Merc, and she might well be happier married to someone of her own background. Perhaps all she had was a crush – love at first sight was pretty unreliable. Sometimes.

'Are you all right, Sophie?'

'Sure. Why not?'

'You sighed as if – you're sure?'

I must have sounded bad for Richard to notice. I pulled myself up and straightened my shoulders. 'I'm fine,' I said.

So I was, compared with Gurjit. Her black clothes hanging drably on her, she leaned against the wall outside the staff room as if she could no longer support her own weight. Her skin was blotchy – from crying if her eyes were anything to go by, though she insisted she merely had a cold when I questioned her.

'My father is right,' she said, pre-empting anything I might have said. 'My college studies must come first. The hours have been over-long, and I'm not sufficiently at home at a keyboard to clear the backlog as quickly as Mark needed it cleared. I let him down – just as I've let you down by pulling out like this.'

I shook my head. 'You stuck at it longer than most. And it sounds as if Mark asked too much of you.'

'I'm afraid his expectations were too high.'

She didn't talk as if she were suffering from a broken heart; but in my experience that didn't mean she wasn't.

'I'll tell you what I'll do,' I said, as if I'd just been struck with inspiration. 'I'll go round to the airport myself tonight and see how much of the backlog I can clear, shall I? And tell him officially that you've left. With a bit of luck he'll be so pleased by the amount we achieved between us he'll give you a smashing reference. Would you want – I could take a message for you.'

She smiled, painfully, shook her head. 'What about that fraud?' she asked, with an obvious effort.

I hoped I'd got away with that. 'Something's obviously been going on. But I doubt it's that serious. I'll talk to him tonight, shall I?'

She lost what little colour she'd had. 'He's bound to blame me . . .'

Logic didn't come into it, did it? And I thought of her parents, and mourned her lost self-esteem.

'He won't.'

'I'd really rather you said nothing – to anyone, Sophie.'

'Not even to the person who I think has been doing it?'

'Could you – really?'

'I've no proof.' With a bit of luck I wouldn't have, anyway. 'But I've got a suspicion. Let me see what I can do.' It occurred to me that there were other people than Richard in the world who might need a hug; I reached up and gave her one. 'Remember: you know where to find me if you need me.'

Her smile was watery, but brave. And then her eyes, catching sight of something behind my back, widened in horror; I turned, following their gaze.

Nothing out of the ordinary, not at William Murdock, deplore it how I might. A young woman dressed from head to toe in black, her face veiled so heavily that there was not more than a two-by-six-inch slit for her eyes. If Gurjit's eyes had been smeared with tears, this woman's were bloodshot with bruising: she staggered, rather than walked, along the corridor.

'Halima!' Gurjit breathed. She turned to me. 'It's Halima. See you later, Sophie.' And she strode off, purposeful again, putting her arms gently round the other woman's shoulders. She glanced quickly back at me. Yes, she knew where to find me. If she needed me.

Having such a splendid young woman putting so much trust in me was scarcely likely to make me feel any better about my criminal activities. OK, there were hundreds of other young women who would benefit from Andy's Third

World work – but I'd spent all my life not only on the side of right but inculcating it into others. If I could get off my high horse and be simply pragmatic it would be better for all concerned. Nearly all. Not the drugs companies, of course, but I found it hard to squeeze a tear for the big multinationals. Their shareholders? Nice ordinary people like me? Surely, a few pence off their dividends wouldn't hurt anyone. I squared my shoulders. I'd whip through the paper records that were left, get them into the post, zap home and spend the night talking to Switzerland. And tomorrow please God, I could start living a normal life again.

Normal. Except for the fact that someone from Andy's past was trying to kill him – and wouldn't mind getting his evil mitts on me. I fingered the canister in my bag.

Chapter Twenty-Four

For once I had an attack of common-sense. There was no way I could work all evening without eating first. And it would give time for the huge traffic tailbacks from Spaghetti Junction to clear from the city centre, which they threatened to gridlock. That nice Italian place called loudly.

The table nearest the bar was occupied by the middle-aged couple I'd seen there before: at least, their coats were draped on their chairs, but they were squatting by the bar. I scanned the menu. Eventually he got up, disappearing into the kitchen, to return with an enormous pair of scissors. She pointed at a weak stem on an anaemic plant; he argued, and pointed to another node. At last, he snipped, she gathered up the foliage, and they both disappeared into the kitchen. I could hear their laughter. Then they returned to their table, arms wrapped round each other, and simply sat, smiling at each other warmly, toasting each other as they sank red wine.

When the chef-cum-waiter asked what I wanted to drink, what could I do? I did what the woman in the movie did: pointed to them, and said, 'Whatever she's having.'

I arrived at the airport early enough to greet one or two of the regular workers leaving: nothing like being brazen. I also knocked at Mark's door, but a passing woman who might well have been his secretary told me he'd been off all day. What did that mean for me? A clearer run – or a constant fear that he was the sort of person who'd make up for a day's absence by turning up in the evening? I thought it safer to assume the latter.

Gurjit had left all the post ready to go out in a laser printer paper box in the corner. It was no problem to fish out the Wednesday invoices, and reprint them. There must have been three weeks' invoices altogether: why couldn't the airport simply have brought in temps to do the job, rather than using unpaid student labour? Although perhaps it was lucky for me they hadn't. But a temp would certainly have been more efficient, and I'd have thought efficiency in collecting money owed to you was one of the essentials of good management. I'd have gone for self-sealing envelopes, too: it'd take me a week to lick this lot. Then I remembered a delight from my own temping days – the artificial licker. Almost certainly it had a more grown-up name, but that seemed good enough to me for a rubber roller that rotated in a bath of water. The desk I was using presumably didn't belong to anyone, so I rooted through it, eventually emerging triumphant. Mindful of all that business about security even when going to the loo, I filled it from a kettle that stood on the window sill. Whoever owned it had the makings of a penicillin farm to rival ours at William Murdock: I suspected the only safe thing to do with the green furry mugs was to bin the lot.

As the printer sighed out invoices, I folded and stuffed and sealed. The folds were probably nowhere as meticulous as Gurjit's, but the pile in the out-tray was growing splendidly. There was no doubt about it – I was winning.

I'd dressed as if for burglary, in the black trouser suit I'd taken to wearing to visit employers whose Asian sensibilities might have been offended by thick tights and miniskirts, so I could have gone for a prowl on the tarmac without being very noticeable. But there was nothing to take me outside. I ought to speed up my stuffing and sticking, and then I could push off and start my Swiss activities. As my hands found a rhythm, my brain went into neutral: a logical place for it to find Andy, I suppose. At least he'd been safe all day. Now the police knew who they were looking for, protecting Andy might become a higher priority. They might even have picked up Malpass by now, so he could euphemistically assist them with their inquiries. I found it in me to regret the passing of the days when the police could be thoroughly unpleasant to a suspect, and then clapped a *Guardian*-buying hand to my mouth. The desire for simple revenge for what Malpass had done to Andy – and me – shocked me. I saw it all over again: the fall, the dreadful broken body. Pete Hughes, caught up in someone else's obsession, someone else's madness. Society would demand its revenge for that, I hoped.

Then I was too busy fending off the spear of pain from my stomach to be vengeful any more. I grabbed two antacid tablets from my bag, but the pain was so vicious I leaned over the pile of post, bracing myself, willing it to clear.

As I did so, the door opened and the lights went out.

I was too slow. He was on me before I could move, grabbing me from the rear in a bear-hug. There was nothing I could do: I was totally pinioned. And the hands were moving across to my chest. And what the fingers were doing to the nipples confirmed what the pressure lower down suggested: that someone was very pleased to see me. Or, rather, Gurjit.

'Mark?' I said, my voice muffled by his arm. 'Please stop that!'

For answer he started to pivot me so he could reach my trousers' zip.

'*Mark*! Stop this, for goodness' sake.'

For answer he fastened his mouth to mine.

My attempts to push him off made him all the more amorous. Then I realised – I was going to be raped. Was this what he'd planned for Gurjit? A rape? Or did she like her sex like this? My God, what a mess.

At last I got a hand free, trying to push it across his mouth. But it was easier to grab his nose, twisting it at first gently and then quite fiercely. He squealed – and I reached for the light switch.

'For Christ's sake, Mark – can't you tell us apart?'

'I thought you'd managed – I thought *she'd* – managed—'

'And Gurjit likes her sex a bit rough, does she? Hell, Mark, she's little better than a schoolgirl! And she's led a very sheltered life.' Irate-teacher mode seemed appropriate. It distracted me from two quite contradictory personal feelings: understandable outrage and a most unforgivable rush of physical desire.

He put his hands to his face and started to cry.

Scrubbing at those disgusting mugs, I had a chance to work out why. Was it sorrow for her? Shock? Fear for his job? Coffee was called for, whatever the reason. And a hearty implication that I'd forgive and forget, that he need not worry about my gossiping. I smiled at myself ruefully: it seemed my greatest talent lay in keeping *stumm*.

He'd rearranged his professional dignity by the time I got back.

'Didn't Gurjit tell you she'd asked me to finish off her work? She said she was so embarrassingly far behind she didn't think she could ask you for a reference. She's very conscientious, is Gurjit.'

I plugged in the kettle. It occurred to me, belatedly, that there might be other reasons for the immense backlog than Gurjit's meticulous approach to work. And yet she had stoically – yes, it was more than passively – accepted her parents' decision.

'I just hoped—'

'What for?'

'That they'd change their mind. Or that she'd change hers. You don't think there's any chance, do you?'

'Do you expect an autocratic father, no matter how much he loves his daughter, to abandon his ambitions for her?'

'She thought her mother—'

'She doesn't utter a word of protest. Not in public. And probably not much of one in private.'

'So—' He shrugged, and came to lean on the window still beside me. 'D'you suppose – if I waited?'

Would eighteen months at William Murdock and three years at University make Gurjit more independent? Or would she simply change her mind about him, as one did about one's early loves? I must have been silent long enough to give him the answer he didn't want: his head drooped, like Richard's.

'I'm sorry,' I said. Sorry for everyone. I put my arm round his shoulders.

At last he turned. 'Sorry – about earlier.'

'No problem.' Not for him: I wasn't so sure about myself. My heart felt physically heavy, and I realised my shoulders were slumping like his. I straightened. 'At least all your invoices are done! I seem to work a bit more briskly than Gurjit.'

'Yes. Well. I mean, thanks, Sophie. Really – thanks.'

I had to tell him, didn't I, about the lapse in his security. About the thefts. Warn him somehow. He was a decent man. He wasn't responsible. But I wanted it to be some unknown individual who found a messy little buck stopping at his or her feet.

Mark watched me stir whitener into the coffee. 'That looks disgusting! Time for the pub, I should say.'

I had to make sure.

'I've always wanted to work one of those franking machines. Can I run this lot through first?'

He looked at me in surprise, as well he might, but we turned it into a game – who could put a batch through in the least time – and I had the double pleasure of watching all those nice safe invoices diving into the post bag and seeing his face lighten with laughter.

Neither of us drank enough to risk our licence. We talked about cricket and music – all very low-key – and arranged to meet in the Italian restaurant for a meal one evening the following week. Apart from anything else, I wanted to see if the plant surgery had worked.

Andy was still up when I got back. His face was exceptionally grim.

'They found him – then they lost him,' he said.

'Found—?'

'Malpass. Living and working in Birmingham. And you'll never guess where he was living. Sit down, I'll get you a drink. And some food.'

'I don't want anything. Just tell me!'

He took my arm and drew me to the window. 'You see that house over there? With the "For Sale" sign? Well, he's been squatting there. But that's not the whole of it, kid. Not by any means. Guess how they found out . . . But first of all, you are going to sit down and you are going to eat.'

'But—'

'Take your coat off, wash your hands and go to the table like a good girl.'

'Yes, Mother.'

Smoked salmon, cream cheese, and bagels he'd shoved into the oven to warm. 'Micro-waving them makes them tough,' he said – anticipating my complaints about keeping an oven on at two hundred degrees for however long he'd been expecting me. 'There! Eat and enjoy.' He passed me a tray, and produced a promising-looking bottle from the fridge.

I spread cream cheese on the first of the bagels. 'Right. Pour yourself a glass and tell me.'

'Do you remember asking why Griff wasn't down here? And I said the fuzz had a close eye on me? Well, I found out just how close this afternoon. Those people opposite – the ones Aggie calls the old dears—'

'Yes. The Harveys. The ones who've been having a lot of visitors recently.'

'Not visitors. The fuzz. Surveillance duty. Watching me.'

'You're joking!'

'I wish I were. Apparently they were still acting on the tip-off that sparked all the problems at that hotel.'

'The Mondiale.'

'So they've had these people shacked up with the – the Harveys? – watching your place night and day all the time I've been here. Not when I wasn't, though. Any road up,' he continued, his lapse into Black Country lingo showing how serious he was, 'one bright spark notices that there are one or two rats visiting a heap of rubbish in next-door's back garden and thinks it can't be very nice for the old dears to have rats as neighbours—'

'At last! Half the road's been petitioning the council to do something about that lot!'

'Quite. Well, now something *has* been done. They call in a rat-catcher or rodent operator or whatever: a shortish roundish man I rather took to on sight—'

'You've *met* him?'

'No, I was looking out of the window. Anyway, this van pulls up opposite, so I have a look. And there's this funny little guy looking like an extra from *Wind in the Willows* toddling all business-like round to the back of the Harveys' neighbours' house. And next thing I know he's scuttling hell for leather round to the Harveys' front door, yelling for an ambulance. So out pour half a dozen very tall young men – you should've seen Ratty's face! – all ready to practise their first aid. But, my dear Watson, they were too late, as the subsequent departure of the apparently sick man in a body bag demonstrated.'

'Hang on – all these histrionics are confusing me. The police smell a rat. *See* one. And the rat-catcher finds – a human body? Is that right?'

'Absolutely. And – ' by now his eyes, which had been gleaming throughout, were positively glittering – 'and guess who the body belongs to?'

I shook my head. He swept the wine bottle from the table, and returned it to the fridge. Then he fished out a bottle of Moet.

'The body is – Malpass's!' He prised out the cork. 'There! So I'm a free man! I don't need to be nannied any more! I can go anywhere I want! I can go – home!'

Chapter Twenty-Five

The following day, I had a reflective journey to work. It would have been pointless to rail at Stephenson and her team for their incompetence, but I wanted to scream with frustration. If I was supposed to be alert and on my toes all the time, why shouldn't other people? How on earth could the police have let Malpass squat under their very eyes? No wonder he'd been able to keep an eye on our activities! All things considered it was fortunate that morning that no one changed lanes selfishly or tried to overtake: he might have found a latter-day Boadicea kicking in his lights.

Perhaps Richard sensed my tension: when I went to report the latest development he produced coffee and chocolate biscuits without even asking. He spoke idly about the roads, a leak in the biology lab ceiling – and then we heard screams.

We nearly collided in the doorway, but I was out first, banging at the lift button. When nothing happened, I yelled, 'Call Security! Then use the lift. I'm on my way down.'

A security guard soon joined me outside. It didn't take long to see what was happening; a group of yobs had found a patch of relatively virgin snow and also found someone to roll in it. The girl was white and shaking by the time the man had collared one of the ring-leaders, and burst into tears as I helped her to her feet.

'Does it hurt?'

'Course it bloody hurts! It's bloody freezing me – me you-know-what.'

'What have they done to you?'

She didn't answer for a moment, more concerned with

the arrival of two patrol cars and a panda. Thank goodness for Security. 'I don't want them men to know. It's – it's women's business, like.'

I scraped some snow from the back of her neck. As far as I could see down her coat her sweatshirt was wet. I undid her collar: the front was soaking too.

'Did they put snow up your legs?'

She nodded.

'I'll make sure there's a WPC,' I said. 'They're really good – I promise.'

And then she gripped my wrist. 'They won't want it to go to court, will they?'

'They've got the bloke that did it. They'll soon get his mates.'

'Ah, but there's others where they came from. And the Bill won't be here every day I come this way, will they?' She was shaking again.

At last the police were with us, and I looked for someone sympathetic. I found an avuncular man, who might have had daughters the woman's age.

'Assault,' I said. 'And I'd reckon it was indecent.'

And then I registered two more facts. There was no sign of Richard; and a paramedic unit was hurtling through the car park. I started to run. I remembered all too clearly his shortness of breath, his grey face. *Not Richard, not a heart attack*. Please, God.

'Is he OK? He's a friend of mine!'

But they were too busy to bother with me.

No one spoke to anyone that day without asking for news of him. At last, I couldn't bear the official silence any longer, and I phoned the Principal.

'Forgive me, Sophie, but I must tell you I think you are over-reacting.'

'Mr Worrall, there are some two hundred and fifty people in this college who respect and care for Richard. We all of us need to know.'

'I will ask Personnel to phone the hospital and put a notice on the Staff board.'

'I think I can manage that myself, thank you very much.'

Casualty were happy to tell me that Mr Jeffreys hadn't had a coronary incident, but was under observation for gall-stones. I could visit him later if I wanted.

I wanted.

When I saw him from the ward door, his face unguarded, Richard was wan and miserable. He wheeled to face me as soon as he heard my voice: it was difficult to work out his reaction. But I found myself shaking hands with him and leaving my hand in his long enough for it to become a clasp. Then the conversation turned to prosaic matters: keys, burglar alarms, pyjamas. I'd drop a suitcase before heading off to the meeting of the Midshire Symphony Orchestra's Friendly Society, of which I was a trustee: why did it have to be this evening?

Andy obviously couldn't wait to leave. Although the police had told him to stay put until all the i's had been dotted, his bag stood ready-packed by the front door. Of the man himself there was no sign. I picked up some books, my Discman and a variety of CDs to keep Richard entertained. I'd just locked the house when I remembered I'd still got Chris's little spray in my bag: I fished it out. Might as well put it back now. But I was cutting it fine if I wanted to pick up Richard's stuff, so I slipped it in my pocket. I'd better ignore the message on my answering machine, too. I'd phone whoever it was when I got back: the meeting shouldn't finish very late.

Richard's house seemed gloomier than I remembered it. Sheila had taken all her house-plants and a lot of books, and it no longer seemed inhabited. I gathered his clothes, uneasy at rifling through other people's drawers, albeit by invitation. His socks seemed pathetically small for such a solid man. I could find nothing better than a Tesco's carrier to put them in.

I resumed my journey. Nowhere to park, of course: it's all very well having these mega-hospitals, but the planners never seem to remember the elementary principle that people have to get there and that public transport has never quite recovered from being de-regulated. Another car and I circled endlessly until a Mini sidled out of a child-sized space. Since my rival was a big Vauxhall and I was in my little Renault, there was no contest. But he stayed in the aisle, as if he hoped I'd change my mind.

The curtains round Richard's bed were closed. I assumed tact in the face of bedpans was in order and hovered a little way off.

'He's been taken bad,' said a voice; it belonged to the occupant of the bed I was hovering near. 'Your dad's been taken real bad. Oxygen.'

'*Oxygen*?'

'Giving him oxygen. Look.' He nodded downwards.

There were a lot of feet by Richard's bed. I sat hard on his neighbour's chair. 'How bad? Heart?'

'You'll have to speak up, me duck.'

'Heart?'

'No! Me bronicals.'

'That man – is it his heart?' I had spoken loud enough to wake the dead and a head popped out from the curtains, which were then pushed aside a couple of feet. A spotty male face peered at me. 'Richard says, if you're Sophie, tell her he's all right. Asthma.'

'Is that all?' I was on my feet and through the curtain.

'Been neglecting myself a bit,' Richard said, pulling down an oxygen mask. 'I'm *fine*,' he insisted, although he palpably wasn't.

'Obviously,' I nodded. 'Never do things by half, do you, Richard? A master of bathos, to boot. Two heart attacks in one day and neither's genuine.'

He started to chuckle.

'I'm surprised you didn't fall and break a couple of bones while you were about it. No, you're not supposed to laugh – go on, have a bit more air. I'll hang on until you can tell me how you want them to run William Murdock in your absence.'

The Vauxhall was packed in the aisle when I got back, but there was no sign of the driver. At least he hadn't blocked me in, though a couple of other drivers were hanging round cursing.

Moseley next. And although there were plenty of opportunites for anyone to overtake, the car that had followed me from the car park stuck with me all the way to Aberlene's, where the meeting was to be held. I half-expected the driver to stop and make some derogatory, chauvinistic comment about my driving, but he went straight past.

Shrugging, I rang Aberlene's doorbell. The next three hours were dedicated to finding new trustees for the Friendly Society. The most recent nominations hadn't been the most felicitous choices: they were awaiting trial for fraud, though happily not, as it happened, against us.

The meeting over, I'd got as far as the traffic lights in Moseley when I realised I was being tailed again. Some of Chris's mates in Traffic, no doubt. Well, good for them. This time I'd really irritate them by doing a precise twenty-nine miles an hour. There was a satisfactory tailback by the time I'd reached the Russell Road Island.

Everyone else had overtaken me by Edgbaston Cricket Ground, but the tail remained where it was. By now I was really peeved. I stabbed into third, and felt the car surge. The Montego behind me surged too: in fact, he gained on me. I floored the throttle.

He *couldn't* be going to overtake here! Not here, where the road was narrow – there wasn't even a pavement – and twisting along the high wall of the golf course boundary.

He *was.*

OK. I could handle him. I braked hard, so hard I thought for a moment he might ram me.

But he didn't ram. He cut in front of me so sharply I had to brake to a standstill, to the accompaniment of a nasty scraping noise from my nearside. Then he accelerated hard away. What the hell—? I got out to look at the damage, taking the torch I keep in the glovebox, but I was shaking so much the circle of light jiggled and danced. And then the spread of light got bigger. A car, approaching fast, my side of the road. Heading fast for my car. My legs.

And nowhere to run except that solid wall.

I was on the Renault's bonnet before I knew it, scrabbling

desperately on what had been immaculate paint. Could I risk looking back? Yes, it was the Montego. He'd been round the island. All I had to throw was my torch as the driver lunged out of the door: pity it wasn't bigger and heavier. Big as his baseball bat.

On the roof now, teetering and slipping. I grabbed at the wall, and heaved. Out of training. My arms and shoulders screamed.

The area was wooded: no fairways just here. While the lying snow gave me light, it covered roots and hollows. If I didn't break my leg first he might break his. I could hear if not see the Club House – someone must be having mammoth shindig. Perhaps they'd save me some booze. Perhaps they'd save me full-stop.

He was closer. Very close. Heavy breaths.

As I ran and swerved something banged repeatedly against my hip. I closed my hand on it briefly: Chris's spray. But the brief reassurance cost me concentration. My right ankle twisted and I was down, crashing hard on my arm and shoulder. He was nearly on me! I rolled, like they do in the movies, and grabbed at the spray. Holding it as if it were a gun with a huge recoil I waited until I could see his eyes. And let rip.

Why hadn't I noticed the balaclava? OK, he was choking nicely, but once he got the balaclava off perhaps he'd strip off the irritant too. And it was only a small aerosol . . .

No point in hanging around. Get to the noise, to the people. My arm was too weak to give me proper leverage, but I was up again, trying to hold it with the left hand while I ran. Yes! People behind big windows. The door? I'd never been to the place, I wasn't the golf club type, I'd no idea how to get in.

And he was moving again.

A terrace. A terrace, with empty glasses on the steps. No one there now. No one, except him and me. I banged the window: they waved back. All as happy as newts.

A door. And then he was on me. No baseball bat, but he'd seen the glasses. A pint beer glass, the sort with a handle – he smashed the side off against the wall. A little shield for him, with a good grip. Nothing for me to throw. Nothing to hide behind.

A scream. And another. Mine. I could scream till he got my throat. Kick my shoe off. Watch it break the window. All those men in dinner jackets. All old, all frail, but enough. Not to catch him. But to make him turn tail.

And rich enough to offer me a choice of malts while we waited for the police.

Chapter Twenty-Six

Malpass was in police custody – that was the good news. We were in Rose Road Police Station to hear it.

'Though whether he'll be fit to plead is another matter,' Stephenson said, leaning back in Chris's chair. 'You've got some odd friends, Mr Rivers.'

'Why? What I can't understand is *why*, for God's sake.'

'He's not saying much that makes sense, to be absolutely honest. I thought it might be good if you enlightened us.'

'Does the victim usually have to explain the reason for the attack?' Andy asked. His voice was so quiet and reasonable it was obvious he was trying not to hit her.

'I mean, if you could give us some idea of the line our questioning should take.'

'I've been over this God knows how many times. He was a cousin of a woman I married, who left me for another man. She had a drug habit and died. Though we were no longer together I started my anti-drugs work. Then I suppose the Third World stuff got more important.'

'Has he said anything about wanting to kill Andy?'

She'd have withered me, had not long practice at dealing scathing looks inured me to those from other people. 'His solicitor would scarcely encourage such revelations. He babbles about just desserts. He's using a biblical turn of phrase at the moment.'

'*Pride goeth before a fall and an haughty spirit before* something or other,' I suggested.

'Exactly.'

'My question about killing Andy wasn't as stupid as it

may have sounded,' I said. 'You see, if Malpass knew Andy's routine, he'd know he never went on to a gantry or anywhere dangerous. If Andy had taken that concoction during a performance, all – all! – he'd have had was some visual disturbances and problems with his hearing. He'd have staggered round, as if he were drunk. He'd have looked a complete fool.' Not like the body spread-eagled on the stage.

'Quite.'

'Perhaps he just wanted to grab the headlines with news that I was on drugs again, so I'd lose credibility. Death by a thousand media cuts! But then he did seem to want to kill me – all those flowers and wreaths, for God's sake. And he seemed quite keen to finish Sophie off last night.'

Shuddering, I huddled into my sweater. It wasn't often I took a sickie, but I'd have taken one today – if I hadn't been helping the police, as it were, with their enquiries.

'Perhaps things just snowballed,' Ian put in. 'Oh. Bad choice of word, that.'

We smiled, thinly.

'Whatever his motivation, we shall have to wait – shit, sorry, sir!' Stephenson was on her feet.

'It's OK – it's your case, Diane. Stay where you are.' Chris took a visitor's chair, out of my line of vision.

'Tell me,' I said, 'how Malpass managed to be resurrected. You see, the last I knew was that his body had been found in the house opposite mine and was carted off to the morgue. If I'd known he was up and about again, I'd have been – '

'Scared shitless?' Andy suggested.

'I was about to say, more circumspect. But you're right, too. Seriously, shouldn't I have been warned?'

'Please keep calm,' Stephenson said.

'I think losing one's temper is a reasonable response to nearly losing one's life,' I said, cold and controlled as I was in the classroom. 'Don't you?'

'My officers tried to warn you—'

'*Warn*? Let's get this straight. You believe Malpass is dead. You find on formal identification that it isn't Malpass – do you know who it is yet, by the way? – because he's got the wrong colour hair and is five inches taller. You fail to notify me that the man who's been tailing my cousin and me is still alive and well. Smacks of negligence to me.'

'I understand,' said Chris, making me jump, 'that you were not at your desk at William Murdock and had not notified your line manager where you were. A message was left on your answering machine. Officers were warned to keep a watch on you. We followed you as far as the hospital, but—'

'My line manager knew perfectly well where I was. I was at his bedside, in a ward at hospital. No, you people have put me at considerable risk, and I'm very far from happy.'

The room became icy with tension: there was a terrible silence. Andy stared stony-faced at the floor; Ian, his mouth a thin line of disapproval, stared at a point six inches over my head. Whatever Chris was doing, he wouldn't be beaming encouragement: at least, not at me.

'Do you wish to make a formal complaint, Ms Rivers?' Stephenson asked.

It took courage for her to ask that. She moved her hands to her lap, but I'd already seen her clenching them so the knuckles whitened.

'Not a formal one. I don't want to louse up anyone's career. I'm angry, not vindictive.'

Another silence.

'I think that just about wraps everything up,' Chris said, getting to his feet. 'Are you doing anything for lunch, Sophie?' His tone wasn't especially inviting.

I looked across at Andy.

'I'll be on the M5 as soon as they've finished with me,' he said, the relief in his voice only too apparent.

'Then I've no plans, Chris,' I said.

I'd suggested the Italian restaurant, which was suddenly full of potted plants. I didn't investigate; Chris was too grim for such frivolity.

He waited until coffee before spreading the airport papers in front of me. 'What are these all about?'

'You've been in my room!' Righteous indignation, not guilt: I must keep it that way.

'You didn't want me to see what you were doing on the computer last Friday. You were edgy all weekend. You talked in your sleep – of course I looked.'

'Next time, ask first.' My voice was rational, reasonable – the sort of voice someone innocent would use. 'Gurjit thought her boyfriend might be committing fraud. I checked the paperwork. I found no evidence that he was doing anything wrong.'

'Would the Fraud Squad?'

'I wouldn't think so. Don't you think I'd have told Dave Clarke if I'd had my doubts?'

'Or me. I rather think you did. I'm not sure if a confession made in your sleep would stand up in a court of law, however. Come on, Sophie. Someone's been nicking odd items from the airport on Wednesday evenings for the last eight weeks. If I looked at a print-out today, what would I find? No – don't bother. You're not a good liar. My theory is that you've found out who's behind it and you want to protect this person. I assume you have a very good reason.'

'I also want to stop the crimes,' I said. 'There will be no more thefts – I can guarantee that.

'There's only one person you'd be prepared to do it for. And only one person who'd want quantities of medical supplies. Oh, Sophie.' He put his hands on mine. Anyone watching would have seen him as a lover, but I felt the steel in his grip.

My throat was tight. 'If any restitution had to be made, I would make it.'

'Jesus, Sophie! You haven't this sort of money! Oh, you have, haven't you: George's money. I don't think he'd have approved.'

'I can't think of anything he'd rather it was spent on. Saving the lives of the poorest people in the world!'

'So you've wiped the evidence, stopped the crime, and want Andy to get off scot-free. Wouldn't do his reputation a lot of good, wouldn't it? Funny – he's succeeded all by himself in putting his future in jeopardy where that madman Malpass failed. Ironic, I call it.'

I said nothing.

'What you want me to do is forget it, right?'

'What you have to do is forget it. There's no evidence you can use.' There were still the Swiss files, of course, but I could deal with them tonight; and if I couldn't, I'd bet my teeth that Griff knew a man who could. 'And as you say, a confession I made in my sleep might be a bit suspect.'

'You wouldn't confess while you're awake?'

'What is there to confess?' I smiled blandly and gathered up my things.

He winced. 'So I do nothing and we'll all live happily ever after. Right?'

My insurance policy covered me for a hire-car while mine was awaiting repair. I'd retrieved my tapes, and sat in the rented Fiesta wondering why I felt so miserable. I tried to examine each strand of emotion. Anger. Yes, anger with myself for having been so careless. Chris would always have a hold over Andy now. And me, for that matter. Not that I expected to see much more of Chris. When we'd got to his car, he'd thrust at me a carrier bag containing all the odds and ends I'd left at his place. Fine. I'd post his tomorrow.

I selected a tape at random.

I wasn't weeping for Chris.

I wasn't angry with Chris.

I wasn't weeping for Chris, but at something he'd said: 'We'll all live happily ever after.'

Chris would. Andy would. But what about me? How could I live happily? Chris had been right: there was only one person I'd have lied and cheated for. Andy. And why? Because I was in love with him. Always had been. Because I'd always loved him more than I could ever love anyone else. And now Andy didn't need me any more.

It was a Bee Gees tape. The music started. Voices in close harmony. *We are ordinary people living ordinary lives.*